From Megan Maitland's Diary

Dear Diary,

Shelby Lord is one of the special people in my life. Not just my goddaughter, but a caring, loving soul who deserves all the love a man can offer. My heart is glad that she's found Gray Jackson, even though it meant she hit another dead end on the search for her birth mother.

It says everything about Shelby that this all came about out of a simple act of kindness. While Gray might be devilishly handsome and terribly bright, he really did have his hands full taking care of those rambunctious twins! Heaven knows what mischief would have occurred if Shelby hadn't stepped in. And what a reward—it's impossible not to see how much he loves her. Now, if Garrett can find the peace and love he deserves... Have faith. I think it's all going to turn out better than I could even imagine.

There's never a dull moment around

MAITLAND MATERNITY

Shelby Lord: Is Shelby really staying to help with the children—or does some part of her think there might be some hope with Gray? After all, he'd kissed her...even *after* he knew her painful secret.

Gray Jackson: Watching Shelby with the twins, Gray feels a longing for a child of his own. Family. The ache is real...and it scares him half to death.

Jem and Scout Jackson: The four-year-old twins delight in rattling their uncle Gray at every turn— yet they're as eager as Gray for Shelby to stay. Can they sense how much Gray needs her?

Jim Lattimer: To Gray's potential employer, family is everything. He assumes Shelby is Gray's wife— and the twins are theirs. Will finding out that Gray isn't even married end Gray's career plans?

Jo Leigh

The Trouble with Twins

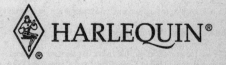

HARLEQUIN®

TORONTO • NEW YORK • LONDON
AMSTERDAM • PARIS • SYDNEY • HAMBURG
STOCKHOLM • ATHENS • TOKYO • MILAN • MADRID
PRAGUE • WARSAW • BUDAPEST • AUCKLAND

HARLEQUIN BOOKS
225 Duncan Mill Road, Don Mills,
Ontario, Canada M3B 3K9

ISBN 0-373-21746-3

THE TROUBLE WITH TWINS

Copyright © 2000 by Harlequin Books S.A.

Jo Leigh is acknowledged as the author of this work.

www.eHarlequin.com

Printed in U.S.A.

A writer of modern fairy tales with sensuality and humor, **Jo Leigh** grew up in Southern California dreaming of making movies. She worked in the film industry for fifteen years and during that time she fell in love with writing. Jo hadn't really thought about writing romance novels, even though her father had been a voracious romance reader for many years. She's written over twenty-five books and writes regularly for the Temptation, American Romance and Intrigue lines. A launch author for the Blaze line, she also contributed to *Trueblood, Texas* and *Heart of the West.* You can imagine how proud Jo's father is of her career at Harlequin! Jo has also taught writing for many years. She lives in Nevada and loves to hear from readers at www.joleigh.com.

To my niece Trysa Shy, who is as loving and kind as she is beautiful. I love you, sweetheart.

CHAPTER ONE

SHELBY PAUSED just before her hand touched the doorbell. What if this was another dead end? What then?

The information Michael and Garrett had given her was sketchy at best. A couple by the name of Jackson had given birth to triplets almost twenty-six years ago. Her brothers hadn't been able to find out the exact date yet. The hospital where Mrs. Jackson had given birth had lost its records in a fire, but one doctor had remembered Mrs. Jackson and the triplets. He'd suggested they come here and try to find out if the Jacksons who lived on this ranch were any relation to the Jackson family with the triplets. It was a long shot. But it was a shot.

The quest to find out what had happened to her birth mother had taken on a new urgency in the past few months. Shelby didn't need a psychiatrist to tell her why. Almost everyone she knew had found someone to love, all in a matter of months. And most of them were already parents or expecting to be parents. Shelby couldn't stop thinking about her own family.

She loved her brothers and sister with all her heart. She harbored nothing but love and respect for her adoptive parents, and she missed them something awful. She loved her diner in Austin, her friends, her apartment. It was all perfect, except for two little details. Thoughts of her birth parents had kept her up night after night. Why had they abandoned four babies? What kind of woman could walk away and never look back? Maybe she couldn't look back. Maybe her note of a few months ago had been sent posthumously. Or as a dying goodbye.

And that other thing? Shelby straightened her shirt and smoothed her hair, then her hand went to her stomach, just beneath her breasts. To the scars…

While there was nothing she could do about that, she could do her utmost to get to the bottom of the mystery of her parents. So here she was. A hundred miles from home, in Blue Point, Texas. Standing on a stranger's doorstep about to ask some very personal questions.

She cleared her throat, prepared to accept whatever was about to happen. But hoping like mad it was going to turn out wonderful.

The doorbell rang loudly enough for her to hear it from the front porch. She expected the door to open immediately, but it didn't. Not even when she rang a second time.

The ranch house was big, though, so it might take someone a while to get to her. Two stories, white colonial, beautiful porch with a double rocker for warm spring nights. The grounds looked well cared for with particular attention paid to flower beds and a small herb garden.

A noise startled her. A bang like a backfire or a gun. Maybe it wasn't such a good idea to show up unannounced like this. She took a step back, prepared to bolt if she had to. The door swung open, and she cringed, waiting for the worst, only mid-wince she realized there was no one at the door. She dropped her gaze and her frightened stance. There *was* someone at the door. She just hadn't expected a preschooler, that's all.

"I hate you!"

Shelby wasn't quite sure how to respond. The little blond boy looked to be about three or four, although the chocolate all over his face made it difficult to be certain. His attire, a rather droopy pair of Toy Story underpants and a T-shirt desperately in need of washing, lent a certain air of nonchalance to the proceedings. She wondered briefly if he was alone in the house. A masculine shout eased her mind. The child hadn't been abandoned. He just wasn't taken care of very well.

"Jem, where are you? Jem!"

Shelby opened her mouth to call to the father, but a howl stunned her into silence. Another child. This one seriously unhappy about something.

The crying got louder as a man holding a second child came around the steps to the foyer. As soon as the little one saw Shelby, she stopped crying. The man, Mr. Jackson presumably, appeared to be in over his head. He also looked to be in his early thirties, which didn't bode well for her purposes.

Shelby had the feeling she'd just discovered the answer to her quest, but she didn't want to jump to conclusions. Maybe he wasn't Mr. Jackson at all. Maybe he wasn't one of the triplets.

He put the child down—a girl, Shelby saw, dressed almost identically to her brother—but before he could say a word, the towheaded child raced toward the stairs, her little legs pumping like pistons. The boy shouted in delight, his dislike for Shelby forgotten, and took off after the girl. The man threw his hands in the air and headed after them. "It's about time you got here," he said over his shoulder. Then he was gone.

Maybe she should come back another time. Say when his kids were in college. But then again, he looked about at the end of his rope. He obviously thought she was someone else. Someone, she assumed, who could handle children. If she lent a hand, he might be more inclined to talk about his family. Even though her hope had dimmed, she *had* come all this way. It seemed prudent to find out what she could. That decided it for her. She stepped inside and closed the door behind her.

As soon as she walked around the base of the stairs she was assailed by chaos. Toys were strewn everywhere, with a preponderance of stuffed dinosaurs and broken crayons. Clothes from long pants to pjs were on the floor, on the tables, and one sneaker perched precariously on top of the wide-screen television blaring Disney's *Pinocchio*. It was a disaster, and from the crying in the other room, she doubted things were going to settle down anytime soon.

"Excuse me?" She walked toward the sound of wailing. "Mr. Jackson?"

He was in the dining room struggling with the little boy. Mr. Jackson, if he was indeed Mr. Jackson, wanted the child to sit down. The child had other plans.

"Mr. Jackson?"

He spun toward her. The little one picked up a spoonful of something white and yucky and threw it on Mr. Jackson's head. "You were supposed to be here two hours ago," the man said, his voice determinedly calm.

"I don't believe I'm the person you think I am."

"You're not from Child Minders?"

She shook her head. "No. I'm sorry to barge in on such a busy day. But I'm here on something of a genealogical quest. Would you—" The screaming went up two decibels. "Would you have a few moments to spare?"

He opened his mouth. Blinked. Closed his mouth. Then burst out laughing. Hard. The little boy stopped crying. The little girl's eyes widened with surprise. Mr. Jackson continued to laugh as he sank down on the seat, unmindful that there was no telling what he was going to sit on.

"Yeah, well, I can see that you don't." She took a step back. "I'm sorry."

He took a deep breath and wiped his eye with his knuckles. "No, hey. My fault. My fault. No problem..."

"Your wife isn't here?"

"I don't have a wife."

"Oh."

He pointed to the boy. "Jem Jackson." Then to the girl. "Scout Jackson."

"As in...?"

He nodded.

"And you are?"

"Their uncle Gray."

"Ah, I see." Being boy and girl, the children were fraternal twins, but their hair was identical in color and texture. Scout's was shaped in what used to be called a Buster Brown, capitalizing on the straight locks. Jem's hair was much shorter, fashionably buzz cut on the sides. Their little faces, dirty and unhappy, were strikingly similar, too. Big blue eyes, pink-tinged cheeks and upturned noses. She'd bet a bundle that when they weren't throwing tantrums, they were downright adorable.

"I know you probably won't believe this," Uncle Gray said, "but I don't have a great deal of experience with children."

"No," she said, feigning disbelief, liking him for his ability to laugh at himself.

"Yes. It's true. I can speak three languages. I won the Long Beach Five Hundred. I've danced a tango with Hillary Clinton. But this—" His hands went up in a gesture of helpless despair. "They've won. I accept my defeat."

"How noble." She stepped over a rocking horse. "But have they eaten lunch yet?"

He shook his head.

She peered at the goop inside the little blue bowl on the Winnie-the-Pooh place mat. "No wonder. That looks awful."

"I know. It tastes worse."

"That's it, then. You need to give them something tasty. Of course, you can't forgo nutrition. But there are lots of things that taste good and are good for them."

His gaze landed on hers, and he studied her for several seconds, reminding her that she was in a strange home, with a man she didn't know. A devastatingly gorgeous man, now that she looked at him, but potentially dangerous nonetheless.

His right brow rose. "I'll pay you a thousand dollars to make them lunch."

It was her turn to laugh. "That's a hefty fee."

"You do know how to cook, don't you?"

"It so happens that cooking is my business. I own a diner in Austin."

His eyes rolled back in sheer gratitude. "Oh, thank God."

"But," she said, picking up the blue bowl, "it's not a thousand dollars that I want in return for my services."

"What? Anything. My car? This house?"

"Nothing quite that expensive. I need time with you. To ask about your family."

"My family?"

She nodded. "I—"

Scout wasn't interested. She was hungry. And her piercing cry brooked no quarter. "I want *pizza!*"

"I'll make food now and talk later."

He nodded before he leaned forward and buried his face in his hands.

She felt sorry for him. Tackling one child this age was an exercise in stamina, but two? She gathered a few other plastic dishes then went through the swinging doors into the kitchen. It was neater in here. The oatmeal box was out, the milk carton, too, and the can of coffee was open next to the pot. Nothing a little spit and polish wouldn't take care of. But first, lunch.

In the refrigerator, she found eggs, milk and butter. Along with the bread on the counter, it was all she needed. Oddly, there was a large assortment of sauces and condiments on two racks, but then, this was Texas. She didn't see many fresh fruits or vegetables, though. With two youngsters, that wasn't good. She took out the ingredients she required.

The battle continued outside. She heard Gray Jackson's calm, reasoned voice as he tried to inform the children that lunch was coming soon. Shelby was no expert on child care, but she did know that when hunger struck, reason had no foothold.

She got to work. Instead of scrambled eggs or French toast, she decided to be a tad more creative and make them something she'd liked as a child.

As she cooked, her thoughts shifted from the children to Uncle Gray. Interesting eyes. They were like his name. More gray than green or blue. But they weren't dull. On the contrary, she saw intelligence there. And humor. Which was right up there on top of her hit parade.

Shelby had always been wildly attracted to men with dark, thick hair. Add his angular nose and chin, pecs to swoon over and a butt made for jeans, and she was practically a goner. Not that she could ever get a man like him. But it didn't hurt to dream, right?

What was this man Gray doing alone with his niece and nephew? Where were their parents? Whatever the situation, it really was none of her business. Except that Gray Jackson was more than likely one of the triplets Mrs. Jackson had delivered, which meant this was, after all, another dead end. She wasn't going to find any answers here. Still, it wouldn't do any harm to ask.

She turned down the flame under the eggs. He certainly was tall. Over six feet. And in wonderful shape. She'd checked out his shoulders as he'd sunk in his chair. And checked out other things as he'd walked toward the living room. Very, very delicious. And, undoubtedly very, very taken. A man like that wouldn't be alone. And even if he was…

"You almost done in there?" Gray called from the living room. "The natives are about to revolt."

"One second. Tell them to sit at the table."

"Right."

She heard an impressive whine, something along the lines of, "I don't wanna." The crash of a chair tipped over, which explained the sound she'd heard at the front door, followed by childish laughter. These kids needed lunch, a bath and a nap.

She put the fried eggs on one big plate, then used Cheerios and shredded wheat to make faces with the eggs as eyes. She picked up two small plates as she headed toward the danger zone.

The children were sitting. And so was Gray. Only they were all on the floor. "Is that where you want to eat?" she asked.

The kids screamed, "Yes!"

"Then that's where you shall eat." She put the big plate between them and gave them a second to look at it.

Scout pointed. "It's a clown."

"It's a big poop," Jem countered.

"It's lunch," Gray said, his voice as weary as the sigh that followed. He looked at Shelby and tried to smile. "Jem is big on poop these days."

"So I gathered."

"His mother says it will pass."

"Everything does." She crouched beside them, grateful she'd worn jeans instead of a skirt, and served each of the kids one egg and split the cereal between them. They tackled the food as if they hadn't eaten in a week.

Gray stood up, watched the children for a moment, then turned to her. "Thank you."

"You're welcome."

"You want some coffee?"

"I'll get it. You sit down. How do you like it?"

"Hot," he said. "And black."

She nodded, then went to the kitchen.

GRAY STARED at the swinging doors as they swayed on the hinges. He always felt like a cowpoke at his brother's. At least the urge to bolt had left with the propitious arrival of the redhead from Austin. Her hair was an interesting color, a mixture of copper and rust and gold. He liked that she wore it down past her shoulders so it swayed, too.

She had nice eyes. Wide. Green. Filled with amusement. It didn't even bother him that her amusement was at his ineptitude. What in hell had he been thinking? No way he should be taking care of these kids. Someone would end up in the emergency room before he was through, and that was the last thing Ben and Ellen needed.

The woman came back carrying two cups of coffee. He took a moment to check her out. A little rounder than he was used to, but nice. An hourglass shape that would have knocked them dead in Marilyn Monroe's day. She put her coffee down first, then turned the other cup around so he could take it by the handle. Her nails were painted the same color as her hair. "Did you tell me your name?"

"I don't think so." She sat across from him. "It's Shelby. Shelby Lord."

"It's a real pleasure, Shelby. You couldn't have come at a better time. Another few minutes and I would have raised the white flag."

She smiled, her lush lips curving easily over straight, white teeth. "So how did you end up in this mess?"

He shook his head. "I was a fool. An arrogant idiot. I didn't know, honest. I haven't been around kids much. Especially not twins. And certainly not on my own."

"Their parents?"

"My sister-in-law, Ellen, had to go see a specialist in Dallas."

"She's ill?"

"Yeah. But it's not dire. Not yet. And now it looks like things are going to be fine."

"That's wonderful."

"I thought so. Which is why I said I'd watch the kids." He sighed again. Sipped some coffee. "I've been staying here for the last couple of months, although this is my first time watching the kids by myself. Ellen and Ben made everything look so easy. Ha."

"So you're not from here?"

"Originally, yes. But I've been away for years. Los Angeles, mostly."

"Ah, but you've come back to your roots, eh? Home to stay?"

He shrugged. "Maybe. If I get the job I'm hoping for."

"What's that?"

"Marketing. There's a company out here, Lattimer Spices. They make barbecue rubs and specialty sauces. They're going national and they need someone to head the operation."

"That explains the racks of jars in the fridge."

He winced. "I'm supposed to go to the grocery store."

"It might be a good idea."

He shook his head. "I called a service and hired a baby-sitter. She was due here at eight this morning."

"She didn't call you?"

"Not a word."

"Maybe something happened. You might call them and see."

"I would. Except I can't find the phone."

"Oh."

"Let me rephrase that. I can't find any of the phones."

She nodded. "I see."

"I imagine you can. It's been…" He didn't finish. It was obvious what his day had been like. The house had been immaculate before Ben and Ellen had taken off. Everything in its place. They'd made it sound like a piece of cake. Feed the kids, play games, maybe a nap. They should have warned him. But then Ben probably thought it was a big joke. "My apologies. You haven't caught me on my best day."

Her smile stayed generous. "No problem. But now that we have a moment, I'd like to ask—"

"The genealogy question."

She nodded. "You're one of triplets, aren't you?"

He nodded, wondering where she'd gotten her information. And why. "I have a brother, Ben, and a sister, Kate. Ben's the oldest, but— Never mind. It's triplet stuff. You wouldn't understand."

"Want to bet?"

"Are you kidding?"

She shook her head, making her hair shimmer.

"Is that what your study is about? Triplets?"

"In an indirect way. I am a triplet. I have a brother, Michael, and a sister, Lana."

"I haven't met many."

"Me, neither. Lots of twins, though."

He shook his head. "Twins. They think they've got problems. They don't know the half of it."

"Well, perhaps they don't know one third of it."

He grinned. "Right. So, what is it about my being a triplet that brought you here?"

Her smile faded, and her gaze went past his shoulder to the far wall. "We were abandoned as infants, along with my older brother, who was two. My brothers are trying to find out who our birth parents are. We've got records of about five triplet births around that time that match our configuration—two girls, one boy. The only couples left to check were your parents and one other. Your hospital records were lost, so we didn't know for sure what the sexes of the triplets were—or even the exact date of birth. Obviously we're down to our last possibility."

"I'm sorry I can't help you. My mother died a year ago. My father still lives here in Blue Point. This was their house. We go back three generations." He looked at Jem, who was picking up Cheerios from the floor and shoving them into his mouth. "Four generations now."

"I figured as much. Not the generation part, but the parents part. It was a long shot, believe me."

"I wish I could give you something. You really saved my life."

She put her cup on the table and gave him a troubled stare. "What about my thousand dollars?"

"Your thou—"

She laughed. A terrific sound. Not a trace of self-consciousness, not at all girly. She laughed like a woman ought to.

"Very amusing."

"Couldn't resist." Her gaze went to the twins. Scout had abandoned her meal and was trailing egg yolk across the wooden floor.

Gray watched as the little girl picked up a broken crayon and stuck it in her mouth. "I'd better get going. I have to give them a bath, go to the market, clean up in here…. Oh, hell." He turned to her, making himself look as pathetic as possible.

She stood up. "Stay right there." Then she walked out of the room.

Jem had grown bored with the cereal and had moved over to the box of Lego by the staircase. Scout was still sucking on her crayon. Gray didn't understand how parents did it. How they got anything done.

He heard the front door shut. Damn. She'd probably taken off for the hills. He didn't blame her. What a mess. What a joke.

But then he heard the door again. Her footsteps. She rounded the bend and smiled as she neared him. "Here."

In her hand was a cell phone.

"Pardon?"

"To call the baby-sitter."

"Oh, right." He closed his eyes for a moment as he cursed his own stupidity. "Thanks."

"What's wrong?"

"Nothing. Except I have my own cell phone in my room."

"Does it work?"

"It works."

"Oh." She sat again.

He went into the kitchen and grabbed the notepaper from behind the hamburger magnet on the fridge. As he dialed the agency, he walked to the dining room. A woman answered on the third ring.

"This is Gray Jackson. You were supposed to send a baby-sitter here this morning."

"Oh, Mr. Jackson. Thank heavens. We were about to call the police."

"Why?"

"We've been trying to reach you all morning, but your phone isn't working."

"Right. We're on it. Now, about the baby-sitter?"

"I'm sorry, we've had a little emergency here. Beth Ann has gone into labor."

"Beth Ann?"

"The woman who was going to help you today."

He thought about that for a moment. "Can she come tomorrow?"

The woman paused for a really long time. "She went into labor to have a baby, Mr. Jackson."

"Oh. Right. And I suppose there's no one else who could—"

"I'm terribly sorry."

"Sure. Thanks anyway." He pushed the off button and handed the phone to Shelby. She seemed very sympathetic. "Please stay. Not forever, but at least for today. I'm desperate."

"Stay? Me?"

He could see the idea hadn't occurred to her. But it was the only solution. "I'll really give you that grand if you agree. I'm drowning here. Going down for the third time."

She eyed him carefully, then slowly looked around the room.

He stayed busy making a bargain with the big man upstairs.

"I can't stand it," Shelby said as she took off after Scout. "Let's get them bathed and down for a nap. We'll negotiate the rest later."

He held back his whoop of joy, said a silent thanks and concentrated on getting Jem away from the mess on the floor and into the downstairs bathroom. What got him was that Shelby had no trouble. Scout went quietly, like a civilized four-year-old. Jem, on the other hand, squirmed like a trout and yelled as if he was being drawn and quartered.

The plain truth was, he had no aptitude for children. They scared him spitless.

He followed Shelby through the living room, rather enjoying the rear view. Not enough women these days had those kind of curves. But, and this surprised him more than anything, it was her kind eyes and gentle smile that made him damn glad she'd decided to stick around.

Aside from the fact that she knew what the hell she was doing.

CHAPTER TWO

SHELBY PUT IT in gear. First, she assessed the situation. Gray was pretty hopeless. Not that he wasn't trying, but he was as comfortable with the children as she'd be with wild badgers. And of course, the children sensed it and acted out. Jem in particular seemed determined to rattle Gray at every turn.

She shouldn't be amused by all the shenanigans, but she was. The twins were just too clever and adorable, and Gray? It was something to see a man like him completely discombobulated. Everything about his clothes, his hair, his manner told her he was rarely out of control. She could imagine him with presidents and movie stars. But when Jem stuck his finger in Gray's ear, the man was shocked insensible. He stammered, blinked, his cheeks turned bright pink, and all in all he made her melt like ice cream in September.

But she'd think about that later. Much later. When she was in the car. At home. At the diner. Oh, yes. If nothing else, this excursion was going to feed her fantasies for a good long time. Which could be pretty depressing if she let it be.

"Uh, Shelby?" Gray said from behind her. "Can they do this bath thing by themselves?"

"Not entirely. You need to be there to supervise."

He stopped in the middle of the long hallway. "Supervise?"

She held back a grin. "It'll be okay. Just remember to breathe deeply."

"Oh, man."

"If you'd rather clean the house and get their clothes together, we can trade."

"No. I can do the bath thing. I hope."

"I have complete faith."

As they stopped at the bathroom door he gave her a look. A suspicious look with one brow raised. "Are you making fun of me?"

She nodded. "Oh, yes."

"Great."

She slid by him and put Scout down. It was all so odd. She felt exhilarated. Supercharged. As if the very air was filled with electricity. She didn't want to leave the room. But the house was a disaster area, and if there was one thing she was good at, it was whipping a place into shape.

She turned on the water and made sure the temperature was right, then plugged up the tub. When she straightened, Gray had stepped back, his face a study in trepidation.

"Jem," she said calmly, "Scout, you two know how to take a bath, right?"

"Yes!" they said simultaneously, with incredible vigor.

"You promise to wash behind your ears?"

"Yes!"

"And wash between your toes?"

"Yes!"

"And wash your hair?"

"Yes!"

She nodded. "Excellent." She turned to Gray, who appeared a little more at ease knowing he didn't have to do quite so much. Still, he looked like he needed a pep talk. She opened the linen closet and took out two nice bath towels and two washcloths. "It's easy," she whispered as she moved next to him to hand him the towels. "All you have to do is make sure that nobody drowns, that the water doesn't get too cold and that they play nicely."

He sighed, relaxing a bit more as his duties were explained.

"Then you dry them off by wrapping them in the towels. By then, I'll be back with their clothes."

"Clothes?"

"They can dress themselves."

"Okay."

She slugged him in the arm. "Buck up, soldier. I know you can handle it."

He tried to smile. He didn't succeed.

She left him there even though it was the last thing she wanted to do. He pulled at her somehow. Drew her to him with his palpable charm. And his vulnerability. It was the mixture, she figured, that made him so compelling.

When she got to the living room she did a quick survey. It was her first real look at the place, and only now did she see how beautiful it was. At least it would be when she got finished.

The living room was very large, white with pale peach trim, bleached wood floors with a multicolored rug under the leather couch. Gray's brother and sister-in-law had done wonderful things with the walls. Three-dimensional art made of wood and rope and other natural materials tied everything together. The plants, mostly ferns, added even more life.

But all that wonderful decor was buried under a

couple of feet of junk. She rolled up her sleeves and dove in.

By the time she'd collected all the toys and dirty clothes, she figured Gray was about ready for her help. After depositing the clothes in the utility room, she went in search of the kids' room. It was upstairs, and it was a honey—one of those theme bedrooms she'd seen in magazines, the teddy bears' picnic. The mural on the wall made her eyes pop with the bright colors and lovely details. The beds were made of thick wood, like slender tree trunks. The toy chest matched the wall, as did the dresser. How lucky Jem and Scout were to grow up here.

She found their clothes easily enough and was careful to pick out distinct styles for each child. A thump made her pause, then hurry downstairs.

She opened the bathroom door and stopped dead. Gray was on the floor, on his knees, right next to the bathtub. His sleeves were rolled past the elbows, and he had each hand on a child's head, shampooing them at the same time. The kids were all smiles.

The floor had big wet spots, as did Gray's shirt and pants, but it was altogether a picture of family bliss. "I can see you've got your hands full."

He turned to her, and for the first time since she'd arrived, he seemed comfortable. "Did you know this stuff doesn't burn if it gets into your eyes?"

"Yep."

"Why don't they do that with regular shampoo?"

"That, I don't know." She walked in and sat on the commode. "You guys look like you're having a good time."

Jem held up a green plastic frog. "I got this."

"Very nice. What's his name?"

"Frog."

"Ah."

Then Scout held up a small blue whale. "His name is Bobbo."

"It is not," Jem said.

"It is so."

"Not."

"So."

"Kids!" Shelby got their attention, then smiled. "Did you wash behind your ears?"

They both nodded, dislodging Gray's hands, which he rinsed before he stood up.

Scout slid under the water and came up sputtering but shampoo-free. Jem did the same a moment later. Gray shook his head at his wrinkled, wet clothes, and Shelby handed him one of the towels. Together, they dried the children and helped them dress. Shelby did the honors with the hair blower while Gray rinsed the tub.

The whole time, the kids chattered like little monkeys. Jem told her all about X-men. Scout had strong opinions about Barbie. And Shelby found herself wishing this was her life. That they were her twins. That Gray was her husband.

But, of course, it was all an illusion. A side trip from her real life. A brief, shimmering moment.

She sighed as she came back down to earth. "They're—" She froze as her gaze went to Gray's chest. He'd unbuttoned his shirt halfway. She could see a light sprinkling of dark hair on a chest so perfect it made her teeth hurt. Shelby felt her face go hot as she caught a glimpse of his nipple.

She jerked her gaze away, appalled at the turn of her thoughts. Good grief, she'd seen men's chests before. And even though his was spectacular, there was no reason for her imagination to take her right to the bedroom. As if that were even in the realm of possibility.

"Did you say something about bed?"

She froze. "What?"

"A nap for the kids?"

"Oh. Yeah." She rolled her eyes at her faux pas. "But I'm thinking it's not going to happen right away."

His gaze went to the youngsters, who where engaged in a contest to see who could make the most horrible face. "Right. So what's the plan?"

"You get Jem, I'll take Scout. Maybe we can find a movie they'd like to watch."

"*Pinocchio!*" Scout shouted.

"*Lion King!*" Jem shouted even louder.

Gray grinned at her as he grabbed Jem by the waist and hauled him over his shoulder.

Shelby caught the look of jealousy on Scout's face, so she bent down, caught the little one by the waist and hoisted her up like a sack of potatoes. Laughter echoed off the bathroom walls as she turned to head for the living room. After her first step, Scout grabbed hold of the bottom of her shirt.

Shelby knew what was going to happen seconds before it did, and there was nothing she could do short of dropping Scout on her head. Small fingers pulled the shirt up all the way to her bra.

Shelby turned to hide her back, but it was too late. Jem's revolted "Eww" said it all. So did Gray's sharp intake of breath.

"Hush, Jem," Gray whispered.

All Shelby wanted to do was disappear. She lowered Scout to the floor, then tugged her shirt into place. Why had she worn this stupid blouse? Why hadn't she worn her yellow top, which she tucked into her pants?

"Shelby?"

She ignored Gray's tentative query. She didn't want to explain about the fire. About the skin grafts. About the scars. "So which is it going to be?" she asked, forcing her voice to sound light and unconcerned. "*Pinocchio* or *Lion King*?"

The ploy worked. Scout raced out of the bathroom, and Shelby followed. The footsteps behind her told her Gray had put Jem down. By the time she reached the end of the hall, Scout and Jem were already at the VCR.

She walked a little faster, but it was no good. She felt him behind her even before he put a hand on her shoulder. She tried not to flinch.

"Shelby."

"Look, Gray. I really do have to be going. I'm supposed to be on vacation here." They reached the living room, and she turned to face him, determined not to let any of her roiling emotions show. "I wonder if you could point me to a place to stay for the night. Preferably something close to a restaurant."

He looked at her for a long time. To his credit, his gaze stayed on her face. It didn't wander to her waist, which was mostly what happened when someone saw her scars. She pretty much ceased to exist as a person. She became a fire victim, a giant scar.

"You don't have to go," he said, his voice so gentle she felt stabbed.

"I do, honestly. I do. I've had a good time here,

though, and I assure you, you'll do fine with the children. They're good kids."

The way he looked at her told her that he wanted to ask but he wasn't sure he should. That was the problem. No one was ever sure.

"So, um, is there a hotel?"

He nodded. "In town. The Blue Point Inn. It's a nice place and it has a great restaurant. It's on Main by the movie theater, impossible to miss."

"Thank you." She smiled. "I appreciate you letting me barge in. It was foolish of me to come all this way when the odds were so slim."

"I wish I could have helped."

"I know. But there's still one more name on the list. With any luck, we'll hit pay dirt." Shelby turned and headed for the kitchen to get her purse. She hated walking in front of him. She knew that, now it was safe, he was staring at her back. Feeling sorry for her.

She grabbed her purse from the counter and made a beeline for the front door. She paused, however, when she got to the kids. What a dreamer she was. To have entertained the idea that she could have this. It would never happen. Not in a million years. "Bye, Scout. Bye, Jem. You two be good, okay?"

Jem nodded absently, but Scout came over, hugged Shelby's legs, then looked up with her wide blue eyes. "Bye, Shelby. I liked your eggs."

"Thank you, honey. It was a real pleasure."

The little one's arms still hugged her legs. Shelby moved them, which she hated, but tears threatened. Big, hot, sobbing tears. No way was she going to do that here.

The second she was free, she hurried to the door.

After it was open, she called another goodbye over her shoulder. But she didn't look back.

GRAY STOOD at the window and watched Shelby pull out of the driveway. He'd handled things poorly. He should have— What? Talked about it? Joked with her?

It was the kind of situation his sister knew how to deal with. Kate was always the one who made everyone feel at ease. How she did it was a mystery. Why hadn't he paid attention? Learned something from her?

He knew exactly why. He was too busy thinking about himself. About his women, his workout schedule, his car, his jobs, then more about his women. That's what his mother had meant, of course. Why she worried about him. Because he was a selfish ass. He couldn't even take care of two little kids by himself.

As he headed to the couch, the little wooden boy on the screen sang too loudly even in this big room. Weren't the kids sleepy yet?

See. Right there. He'd done it again. Not two seconds after identifying the problem, he'd gone right back into selfish mode. He wasn't thinking that the kids needed sleep. It was all about him wanting peace and quiet.

He sank onto the sofa and tuned out the noise around him. Damn it, he'd liked her. He'd liked talking to her. What had happened to her? He was pretty sure it was scar tissue from a bad burn. Was it all over her back? All over her body?

He winced, thinking about the pain. About what she'd gone through. It must have been hell. She wasn't bitter, though. Not at all. Instead, she was funny, warm and compassionate. Strange how tragedy affected people so differently. Some turned against the world, and some made the world a better place.

He'd be one of the bitter ones. Especially if he was disfigured. His self-condemnation was interrupted by a small girl climbing on his lap. She smelled like soap and childhood, and for a moment he let himself think only good things.

"Uncle Gray?"

"Scout?"

"Why was Shelby's skin all ugly?"

The good thoughts vanished. "It's different, Scout. Not ugly."

"Why was Shelby's skin all different?"

"I think she was burned, kiddo. It must have hurt a lot."

Scout's brows went down. "Did she play with matches?"

"I don't know."

Scout touched his cheek. Her little hand felt cool and soft, and it was such a spontaneous gesture he had to close his eyes. "She was a nice lady," Scout said.

"She was."

Her hand moved to his lips in a totally guileless gesture, and he kissed her fingers. Scout's smile made him swallow hard.

THE ROOM wasn't large, but it was pretty. From the second floor of the Blue Point Inn, Shelby could see most of Main Street from the window. It was a peaceful little town, like several she knew in this part of Texas. Folks had lived here for generations and would continue to live here for years to come. It was a place to raise children. A place to make a home.

Shelby turned from the window, and her eyes lit upon the phone. She should call the diner. She should call Garrett, Michael, Lana. But she didn't trust her voice. Everyone would survive without hearing from her. Instead, she went to the bed and her suitcase. She'd packed for a couple of days, just in case, and she was glad of it. She wanted nothing more than to climb into something comfy and curl up on the big chair in the corner and read her book. No, that wasn't true. There was one thing she wanted more. She wanted to stop thinking about Gray Jackson.

Her hand went to her stomach before she gripped the zipper of the small suitcase. Once she had it opened, she worked quickly, hanging up what needed to be hung and putting her toiletries in the bathroom. Then she took out a pair of red shorts and a white, oversize T-shirt. She got out of her jeans first, folded them and put them in the case, then she lifted her blouse over her head. She reached for her T-shirt, but her gaze caught on the mirror to her right.

Stopping mid-gesture, she turned to face her image. The scar tissue wasn't too bad around her waist, thighs and chest. Nothing she couldn't live with. Then she turned and looked over her shoulder. The sight made her cringe.

Most of her back was hairless, poreless fake skin. The redness was nothing like before, nothing like when it was new. But there was no way anyone would mistake it for the real thing—it wasn't. It was mostly collagen fibers, not skin cells.

And it was ugly. The kind of ugly that scars the inside, too. The teasing never went away. The way a person's face changed after seeing it was indelible. The fire had taken so much from her.

She closed her eyes as she pulled on her T-shirt. It was enough. She couldn't afford to feel sorry for herself for too long. That led straight into a cycle of depression that scared the hell out of her. If only Scout hadn't—

Her eyelids popped open. The most dangerous words in the English language were "if only." Nothing could be done about the past. All that she had were choices in the now. She could choose to dwell on this or she could opt for healthy, nurturing thoughts.

She pulled on shorts, splashed some cold water on her face and got her book out of her purse. It was a long, juicy novel, one she'd been meaning to read for ages. The author was one of her favorites, which was a good thing. She needed to get lost. To stop being in this world and enter the fictional dream. Damn it, she needed a happy ending.

CHAPTER THREE

SHELBY TURNED THE PAGE and put the edge of her dinner plate on the bottom of the book to hold it open. She hardly looked at her grilled salmon or the baby red potatoes, even though they were quite good. She'd been captured by a quiet cowboy on a mountain in Wyoming. Her eyes skimmed the pages hungrily, looking for the moment when he realized he was in love.

She was the heroine. Just like always.

Someone came into her peripheral vision, and she fought the urge to shoo them away with her hand. It was the waitress. Bella, her name tag read. A nice older woman, and Shelby smiled at her.

"Would you like a refill on your iced tea?"

"Please."

Bella nodded, but Shelby could see her strain to read the title of the book. She flipped it closed, showing the woman the cover.

"Ah, that's a good one," she said. "I wish I could read it again for the first time."

"I know just what you mean."

"You let me know when you want me."

"Thank you." Shelby watched until Bella stopped at another table, then she opened her book once more. She found where she'd left off, and with each line, more of the restaurant disappeared. She could picture the mountain, the sky, the lightning. Mostly she could picture the hero. His gray eyes. His dark, thick hair. His angular nose and chin. His butt made for jeans.

She sighed as she turned another page. A child's giggle, high-pitched, broke into her space, but Shelby pushed it away. She didn't want to listen to children. Not tonight. Focusing more fully, she went back to the book and reread the last line. Once more, the giggle slipped in.

If it was going to be like that, she was going to finish her dinner quickly and get back to her room. It had been ages since she'd stayed up late to finish a book. Too much to do at Austin Eats. But tonight, she was going to indulge herself. A hot bath, a cold drink and her cowboy all night long.

The giggle came again, closer this time. She shoved the bookmark in place and closed the novel. She'd finished over half her meal, which was somewhat surprising. Now to finish the other half and leave.

The laughter commenced at her first bite, and Shelby couldn't stand it any longer. She was going to find the child's mother and give her a stern look. Which wasn't fair. Kids had to eat, too. Hadn't she been concerned about just that a few hours ago? Well, the look wouldn't be *that* stern.

She scanned the tables to her right, but there were no children at any of them. There were three other booths like hers, and she could see two of them. No kids.

The giggle came again. No, wait. It wasn't one giggle. It was two.

She turned slowly until she could see the booth directly behind hers.

Scout and Jem stared over the banquette, grins as wide as the Missouri.

"What on earth?"

"We came to get you," Scout said.

Jem gave her an angry scowl. "You're not supposed to say that."

"I know."

"You do not!"

"Kids," Shelby said, "It's okay." She couldn't see beyond them, but she knew Gray had to be on the opposite side of the booth. She wasn't at all sure how to feel about this. Did he come here out of guilt? Out of pity?

"I'm getting pisgetti," Scout announced, "and Jem's getting a hamburger."

"They both sound delicious." Her neck wasn't going to last much longer in this position. She could turn and pretend to ignore them, but that felt silly. Asking them to join her didn't mean anything. It was only one meal, after all. "Why don't you come here to this table? And you can bring your uncle with you."

The twins scrambled out of the booth and scooted into hers before Gray stood up. He came to her side wearing a sheepish smile. "I know we're intruding."

"It's all right."

"Is it?"

She nodded. It *was* all right. At least, she hoped it would be. The urge to check her T-shirt, to make sure she was completely covered, was more than she could withstand, and her hand went to her waist. Gray caught the action, but he didn't comment. Instead, he scooted in next to Jem.

"How's the salmon?"

"Good."

"It's a pretty nice place."

"Yes."

"The kids haven't been here in a long time, so I thought…"

"It's all right."

He sighed as he shook his head. "I'm sorry. It was a stupid thing to do. I just hated that—" He stopped midsentence.

She had to give it to him, though. Usually when people found themselves in this position, their eyes got all panicky and their cheeks burned with embarrassment. Gray seemed only mildly uncomfortable.

"I hated the way you left," he said finally.

"I didn't mean to upset you. It wasn't personal. I knew you could handle everything and…" She was the one who stopped this time. She couldn't lie. She didn't think he could handle the children all that well, and she wasn't anxious to get on with her vacation. "I left because I was embarrassed," she admitted, utterly shocked at her own honesty.

Gray leaned forward, his hand halfway across the table. "I do understand. You don't know me. But I hope you can believe I wasn't upset. I mean, I was upset because it's clear you were hurt, but I didn't mind." He rolled his eyes. "I'm saying this badly."

"No, you're not. It's a difficult thing to talk about."

"Uncle Gray, can I have a Coke?"

He nodded without looking at Jem.

"Can I have one, too?" Scout asked.

He nodded once more, but his attention never really shifted from Shelby. "Is it uncomfortable for you to tell me what happened?"

"No." She cleared her throat, then shifted on the banquette. "I was nine. It was Halloween, and I was trick-or-treating with my brothers and sister. I was Pocahontas, complete with fringed dress. At Mrs. Winston's house, I stood too close to the jack-o'-lantern, and the fringe caught fire. It happened very quickly. By the time my father raced up and got me on the ground, my back had third-degree burns. I was in the hospital for months. What you saw were skin grafts. All together, I had five operations."

Gray didn't say anything for a long moment. His gaze didn't waver at all. "I'm sorry."

"Me, too."

"I can't imagine it. Literally. I can't conceive of going through something like that and coming out whole on the other end."

Whole? Was she? "You do what you have to do."

The waitress came back, and for the next few minutes, everyone concentrated on dinner. Shelby used the opportunity to audit herself. She wasn't upset. She wasn't even uncomfortable. In a strange way, telling him the story had made her more relaxed. He was so physically perfect she never would have guessed she'd react this way. Usually, when she was around that kind of beauty, she pretended she didn't have a body at all. But with Gray she was incredibly aware of her body and his.

He got to her. He made her fluttery inside, anxious, but not in a bad way. If she was going to be completely honest, she'd have to admit that he turned her on like a radio. None of it made any sense. She'd run from him because he'd seen her scars, so why, just a few hours later, did she feel this intense sexual heat? She wasn't going to sleep with him. She knew, despite his kind eyes, that he would never want her. Evidently, her body didn't care. It was tingling in the most intriguing way.

"So," Gray said the moment Bella left. "I don't want to dwell on this, but I do want to ask you one more thing."

"Go on," she said, her voice uninflected but her insides doing back flips.

"Will you come back? Not forever, but just for tonight? I know you've paid for the room, but I'll take care of that."

She laughed, more with surprise than anything else. "Are you kidding?"

"No." He leaned forward and reached out. "Shelby, please. Look, I know I have no business asking you, but I need your help." He checked Scout and Jem, and they were occupied with the salt and pepper shakers. He lowered his voice so that only she could hear. "I'm horribly inept, and to add insult to injury, scared to death."

"I know you can get through tonight, and by tomorrow, I'm sure you can find someone to help you."

He nodded slowly. "Fair enough. It was a long shot."

She felt badly, especially when he gave her an obviously fake smile.

"So what are you reading?" he asked, his cheery tone as phony as his grin.

She turned the book in his direction.

"Romance?"

She nodded.

"I don't read much of that."

"Really?" she said, moving toward playful, trying to make the dinner as pleasant as possible.

"I should. Probably would explain a lot about women."

"I agree. Frankly, they should be required reading for all men over the age of seventeen."

Little fingers tugged Gray's attention away. "Uncle Gray?"

"Yes, Scout?"

"Can Shelby read us our story tonight?"

He glanced at her, then at Scout. "Shelby won't be there, honey."

"But, you said."

"I know. But she has other things she needs to do."

Scout looked at her. "Do you have other children to take care of?"

The arrow went right into the center of her back. "No, Scout. It's just that... I just..."

"It's okay," Scout said.

Her little face looked genuinely disheartened. Could she really say no to that? Could she be comfortable tonight, knowing Gray was struggling with the kids?

"I want my Coke." Jem stood on the banquette, searching for the waitress.

"Sit down, Jem." She said the words at the same time Gray said them.

Jem sat.

Shelby smiled at Gray.

Gray smiled back.

"Oh, what the heck." She shook her head at her own foolishness. "I'll come. But just for one night."

Gray's smile lit up his face and did something awfully peculiar to her insides. What had she done?

He ended up paying for her dinner. They all went

to her room, and Jem and Scout watched TV while she packed again. Gray offered to help, but she didn't need any. He just kept smiling at her, and frankly, she was a bit disconcerted by the whole thing. Finally, he carried her bags down, insisted on paying for her room, and then walked her to her car. The kids wanted to ride with her, and she let them.

The whole way home, they chattered like monkeys while she kept her eyes on Gray's car in front of her. What on earth was she doing? Driving straight into trouble, that's what.

HE LISTENED to her read the story, although he couldn't have repeated a word. He was struck by the timbre of her voice, the way her whole face got involved in the telling. He wanted her to go on forever, even though the kids were mostly asleep. Jem fought it, but even he couldn't defend himself against her mesmerizing lilt.

Going after her had been the right thing. He hadn't been sure up until he'd seen her face when it was so clear the children wanted her back. Of the three of them, though, he was the one who'd been most eager.

Besides, she was on vacation, right? It wasn't as if he was taking her away from a job or her family. He'd pay her, too, in addition to taking care of her hotel bill.

Was it his fault she'd turned out to be a good cook and great baby-sitter? Or that she was so easy on the eyes? He was just lucky, that's all. Luckiest man in Blue Point.

He stood, and she stopped speaking. The quiet moved in to fill the space, and for a moment he thought about asking her to finish the story in his bedroom.

"What's wrong?" she asked, her voice a low whisper now that the children were finally asleep.

"Nothing," he whispered back. "Why?"

"You looked as if you'd smelled something terrible."

"Nope. Just thinking."

"While you're thinking, come hold Scout while I sneak out."

He went to the bed and scooped a limp Scout into his arms and lifted her off Shelby's lap. It only took a second for Shelby to extricate herself, then push a pillow in her place.

As Gray lowered the little one, he felt a stirring the likes of which scared him half to death.

Longing. Longing for a child. For a baby girl just like Scout. Or a boy. It didn't matter. The longing was there and it was real and he had to get the hell out of the room. If he were smart, he'd get out of the state. Because it wasn't the first time this had happened.

He wasn't ready for children. He wasn't responsible enough to be a father. Hell, he couldn't even feed them lunch. Any kids he had would be ruined for life, destined to spend hundreds of hours on a psychiatrist's couch.

He backed away from Scout's bed as if the proximity to the child was the reason behind this sudden madness.

His elbow hit Shelby, and he jumped, then turned to face her.

Big mistake. She had great eyes. Even better lips.

The sudden desire to explore her mouth, her body, jolted him.

No, no. This was not why he'd asked her back. In fact, if she even guessed at his thoughts, she'd be out of here so fast she'd leave skid marks.

"Is there something else?"

"Hmm?"

She smiled, a little indulgently, he thought. "Is there a reason we're standing here staring at each other?"

"Staring?"

"Yes."

"No."

"No, we're not staring?"

"No, we're not staring for a reason."

She arched her right brow. "Okay. I'm leaving now. You can do whatever you like."

No, he couldn't. 'Cause what he'd like to do was kiss her. Right here. Right this minute.

Shelby headed toward the door, and before he'd moved a muscle to stop her, she was gone.

He sank down on the edge of Jem's bed. What in hell was going on? This wasn't like him. Wanting an attractive woman was pretty much s.o.p. And he did find her attractive. The scars didn't bother him, which actually was something of a surprise. He'd have figured he was too much of a jerk for that. Wonders never ceased.

CHAPTER FOUR

SHELBY WHIRLED, sending the water in her glass flying in the semidark kitchen. "Oh, I didn't hear you."

"I'm sorry. I didn't mean to frighten you."

"I know. You would have said 'boo' if you had."

He grinned that perfect grin of his. God, with that dark stubble of a beard and his tousled hair, Gray looked even sexier. Like *that* was fair.

"I thought you'd be asleep by now."

She shrugged, very aware of the shortness of her sleep shirt. If she wasn't careful to keep it tugged down, he'd see the scars on the backs of her thighs. "I was reading. Then I got thirsty."

He nodded, shuffled barefoot to the fridge and opened the door. The light from inside illuminated the front of him. Every excellent inch. He wore loose striped pajama bottoms and a white T-shirt. On him, it worked.

"Well, I guess I'll be heading back." She was anxious to leave, to be away from his pheromones, or whatever was making her so nuts.

"Don't. Not yet."

There wasn't enough light to see his expression. All he did was confuse her. It was clear he wanted nothing more than to be friends. Temporary friends, at that. Which was fine. Except that she didn't know if she could be friends with him, even for one night.

Every time she saw him her body shifted into sex mode. It was getting rather tiresome.

"Sit with me," he said, his voice husky, as if he'd been asleep. "Talk to me."

"About?"

"Anything. Your family. This mother you're looking for."

"Ah, a light topic."

"It brought you a long way. It sounded like it was important to you."

She had to give him that. It was important. She pulled out a chair and sat while he foraged in the fridge. He ended up with several packages of cold cuts, mustard, cheese, a loaf of bread and a soda.

"So, talk," he said as he sat across from her and began to prepare his sandwich.

She wasn't quite sure where to start. "I called my brother Garrett to tell him what I found. He was pretty upset."

"Aren't you?"

She nodded. "But not as much as Garrett. He's determined to get to the bottom of this little mystery. You have to admit, it's unusual. To leave a child on a doorstep is one thing. To leave four kids is something else entirely."

"Why? It actually makes more sense to me. Your parents might have been able to handle one. But four? That's a lot of diapers and bottles."

"Yes, you're right. But… You see, two months ago, our mother made contact for the first time. Not directly, though. Through a friend. Megan Maitland. You've probably heard of Maitland Maternity in Austin?"

Gray nodded. "The baby on the doorstep thing, right?"

"And not the first baby. That's where we were left."

He put a slice of roast beef on his plate and leaned forward. "And your mother got in touch with you now?"

"She sent some items to Megan. Hand-knitted sweaters for me, Michael and Lana, and an old teddy bear for Garrett. She sent a note, too."

"What did it say?"

Shelby closed her eyes and remembered sitting in Megan's study, hearing her mother's words. "'Dear Mrs. Megan Maitland,'" she began, recalling every word by heart. "'Thank you for finding my babies a good and loving home all those years ago—I knew you would. The teddy bear was Garrett's, and these three baby sweaters have the triplets' names embroidered on them. The only fancywork I ever had time to do. My only wish is for the children to know I loved them. Yours in gratitude.'"

She opened her eyes and gave Gray a small smile. "You can see where it would pique one's curiosity."

"No kidding. So tell me again, how did you end up here?"

"My brother Garrett did some research on triplets born in Texas the same year we were abandoned. They weren't so common then. Not like today with all the fertility drugs. He found five sets of fraternal triplets that could have been us. We decided to look them up, so Garrett and I split up the list."

"What about Michael and, who is it, Lana?"

She nodded. "Lana just got married, and she has

a little one to look after. Michael wasn't very interested at first, not until he got married last month—''

"Boy, this has been some year for you guys."

"You have no idea."

"So who's left? On the list, I mean."

"One couple, by the name of Larrimore. We know the husband's dead, but we have no idea how to contact his wife."

"So you think she's the one?"

"I don't know anymore. Someone sent the sweaters and the bear to Megan. If it was her, she's certainly managed to keep her identity a secret."

"And if it's not her?"

"There's really nowhere else to look. We could have been born out of state, but where on earth would we begin to search?"

"Are you okay with that?"

"I'll have to be, won't I?"

He frowned. "I guess that answers my question."

"I'm sorry. It's just a lot to get used to, that's all. I loved my parents very much. They took us in heart and soul, and we never felt 'less than,' ever. But there is still a part of me that wonders. I'd like to know the answers, but it won't kill me not to know. I've been very lucky all my life."

His gaze darted to her waist, then quickly to his sandwich.

"I know. It doesn't seem very lucky when you look on the outside. But I was. I've had so much joy and so much satisfaction in my life. Only—"

"Only?"

"Nothing. It doesn't matter."

"Sure it does. Come on. Spill."

"Nothing every other single woman my age hasn't

felt," she said, trying to make things light. "I'd like to find someone. Get married. Have children."

"Ah, that."

"Yes. That."

"It'll happen for you, Shelby. I know it will."

She felt her face flush, knowing he was just saying the words, not meaning them. "It's time for me to hit the sack." She stood up and got her water glass. "Enjoy your sandwich."

"Shelby?"

"Hmm?"

He shook his head. "Nothing. Sleep well. I'll see you in the morning."

She left him in the kitchen and went to the guest room at the back of the house. It was cozy and nice, with a little TV set and a great selection of books and magazines, as well as a very comfortable bed and an attached bath.

She wasn't sorry she'd come back. Not really. But she did wonder if she'd come for the right reasons. Was it really to help with the children? Or did some part of her think there might be the possibility of a tango or two with Gray?

If she harbored even the slightest hope, she'd better get the heck out of here as soon as possible. No way anything was going to happen. No possible way.

Daydreaming was one thing. False hope was something else. Something dangerous. If she wasn't careful, she was going to get burned again. And she already had too many scars.

THE NEXT MORNING, she found Gray in the living room, on the floor with Scout and Jem. The three of them were digging through a huge box of Lincoln Logs as if searching for buried treasure.

"Having fun?"

Gray raised his gaze, though not his head. "My car keys."

"Ah. Well, they'll turn up."

"Right."

She grinned and left them to it. She'd decided to make French toast for breakfast. If they had syrup, that is. If not, she'd wing it. Surprisingly, she'd slept well, and woken happy despite yesterday. Or maybe because of it.

The syrup was in the cupboard, and she went about preparing the meal. As she put the first slices of bread in the frying pan, she realized she was humming. It was as if she was playing house, just like when she was a kid. Only this time, the playhouse was a ranch, the kids were real, and the daddy made her break out in a cold sweat.

Just so long as she remembered it was make-believe, everything would be fine. Besides, she wouldn't be here long enough to get into serious trouble.

She considered heading to Dallas. It had been on her mind on the drive here, and the thought of a nice little vacation certainly had appeal. It had been too long since she'd taken off. Forgotten about the diner, about her busy life in Austin. So much had happened recently it had made everything intense.

She thought about the drama of the last year. Sara—no, her name wasn't Sara. It was Lacy Clark. Wrong again—Lacy O'Hara now. How strange that had all been. Amnesia, missing babies, kidnapping plots…it was still hard to believe. But it had all turned out for the best. Except Lacy wasn't the chef any-more, and Mary Jane had left to raise her baby. Truth be told, it was a little lonely at the diner. Even though she liked the new staff very much, it just wasn't the same.

She sighed as she turned the French toast. Some-thing was going on with her. She'd known it now for over a month. She'd been waking up in the middle of the night. Forgetting things. Daydreaming far more than usual, which was really saying something. Maybe it was just that everyone else was getting mar-ried and having babies.

Why it should bother her, she had no idea. She'd reached one of her goals, hadn't she? At twenty-four she'd bought the diner. It was a smashing success, and she had every reason to be proud. Garrett, Mi-chael and Lana had all helped, of course, but for the most part, she'd done it on her own. A dream fulfilled.

But she'd also dreamed that she'd be married by now. In the perfect version of her life, she'd have married at twenty-five, become pregnant at twenty-six and then again at twenty-eight. She'd have a boy and a girl. Maybe even twins. She'd have a house with a big backyard, with swings and a pool. Her husband would help her with the children, not be-cause he had to but because he wanted to.

Her husband would love her, and in his eyes, she'd be beautiful. He wouldn't mind about the scars. He would hardly see them.

It was all so clear to her, and had been for as long as she could remember. The thing was, she hadn't made one move to make the dream come true. When was the last time she'd been on a date? Years ago.

That made it very difficult to fall in love, let alone the rest.

If she didn't do something soon, she was going to have to settle for phase one and only phase one. Heck, maybe that's all she was ever supposed to have. But could it make her happy for the rest of her life?

GRAY FOUND HIS KEYS. Of course they weren't in among the Lincoln Logs. They were under the couch. Right next to the telephone. Or, he should say, the pieces of what used to be a telephone. Little monsters.

He frowned at Scout. It turned out to be a big mistake. Her bottom lip quivered, her eyes filled with tears, and then she started bawling as if he'd busted her balloon.

He scooped her up in his arms and took her to the couch, keeping her in his lap as he sat down. "Hey, Scout."

She cried some more, although he thought he detected a pause.

"Scout, honey, please don't cry. I didn't mean it."

She sniffled. He realized she needed a tissue. He shuddered but kept on smiling. He loved Scout. Really. But jeez, she was so...untidy. And Jem was twice as bad.

He hadn't thought this through. Not all the ramifications. When Ben had asked him to watch the twins, he'd figured it would be tough but nothing he couldn't handle. How wrong he'd been. But that wasn't the big issue now. He carried Scout into the kitchen and pulled a tissue from the box on the counter. Holding it to her little nose, he said, "Blow."

She did. Fiercely. She screwed up her face and

blew through her nose and through her mouth. It was actually kind of cute—in a semidisgusting sort of way. Unfortunately, Scout continued to pout.

"What's wrong?"

He looked over his shoulder to see Shelby's concerned gaze on Scout. "She thinks I'm mad at her."

"Why would she think that?"

"I frowned at her."

Scout nodded, sniffing harder.

"Hmm." Shelby came close and stood right beside him. "Honey, Uncle Gray was just teasing."

"He's mad at me."

"No, he's not."

"No, I'm not."

"He is so. He said a bad word."

Shelby folded her arms across her chest. "A bad word, eh?"

"He said shit."

Shelby pressed her lips together so she wouldn't laugh. He wasn't so successful. But he quickly turned his laughter into a cough.

"It's not funny," Shelby said. "Scout, sweetie, I know Uncle Gray didn't mean to scare you. He's sorry he said that word, and he won't do it again."

Scout wiped her nose on her arm, and despite the recent use of a tissue, it wasn't pretty. "Can I have juice?"

"Of course." Shelby held out her hand, and he set Scout on the floor. The girls went to the fridge while he headed to the living room.

He settled on the couch, and as he put the phone back together, he wondered what it was about Shelby that made her so comfortable. He'd never felt such immediate trust for another person. She had the kids eating out of her hand. He'd lucked out incredibly. Perhaps he could convince her to stay until Ellen and Ben came back.

Just as he screwed on the last piece of the phone, the doorbell rang. He got up, but Jem was running full speed ahead. The doorbell was big around here, right up there with dogs barking and phones ringing. By the time Gray got to the door, it was already open. A man, a big man, stood on the porch smiling at the boy. Gray knew him. He just couldn't remember in what context. A friend of Ben's, maybe? A neighbor he'd seen on a previous visit?

"Gray Jackson?"

"That's right."

The man thrust out a beefy hand. "Jim Lattimer here."

"Jim..." Gray snapped his hand out for a firm shake. "How do you do, Mr. Lattimer. I didn't expect—"

"I know that. And I don't make it a habit of dropping in on prospective employees like this. But I couldn't reach you on the phone."

"Right. The twins."

"There's another one like this?"

Gray nodded. He felt completely off guard, unprepared and vulnerable. What he had to do was calm down. Breathe. Get himself together. "He's got a sister."

"I'll bet she's just as cute as can be."

Gray smiled, then jerked back a step. "Come in."

"Thank you."

Jem stared at the big man. Lattimer was at least six five and maybe three hundred pounds. He was solid as a rock, like a football player or a refrigerator.

"As I said, I couldn't reach you on the phone, and I was in the neighborhood, so I took a chance on finding you home. If it's not a good time, I can turn right around again."

"No," Gray said, leading him into the living room. "It's fine. Fine. Come on in. Have a seat. Can I get you something to drink?"

Lattimer swallowed. "I'd be grateful. I've been on the road since six this morning without a break. Had one of those gas station cups of coffee. It was hot, which is about all the good I can say about it."

"Water or—"

"Water will do nicely," Lattimer said. "For a start."

"Great." He headed for the kitchen. Lattimer started talking to Jem, and Gray moved faster.

Shelby was at the sink. Scout stood next to her, a square box of juice in her hand.

"What do we have to drink?"

Shelby turned at the sharpness of his voice. "Not much. Water. Coffee. Juice."

"No beer?"

"I don't know. Why?"

"Lattimer. He's here."

"Pardon?"

"Jim Lattimer. The man I'm supposed to be interviewed by next Monday. He dropped by."

"Oh, dear."

"Yeah. And from the looks of him, he's hungry. I know he's thirsty."

"Uh-oh."

"Yeah."

She turned and poured a glass of filtered water, then handed it to him. "Stall him."

"Stall him?"

"Go!"

Gray nodded, then headed toward the CEO of Lattimer Spices, Inc. Damn it, Gray's clothes were a mess. His hair—oh man, who knew what that looked like. Of all the damn times to—

"There you are," Lattimer said, his voice deep and booming. He grinned as he took the glass, then downed the liquid in several large gulps.

Jem's mouth hung open at the sight.

"What's wrong, young man? Haven't you ever seen a thirsty fella before?"

Jem shook his head, his gaze not leaving the big man's face. Lattimer laughed. "You should see me eat!"

"Jem, why don't you go find Scout? I think she's in the kitchen."

It was clear Jem was far more interested in the strange man. But when Gray gave him a private glare, Jem got moving.

"Great kid," Lattimer said. "Great. But I know you don't want to talk children. You want to know what the high heaven I'm doing here on this fine Tuesday."

"Yes, I was curious about that."

"Sit down, son."

Gray obeyed, sitting across from the couch.

"I'm here because I like to meet the people who want to work for me. Meet 'em away from the office. See what they're like in the real world."

"That makes sense."

"It does. Especially in view of the considerable financial risks I'm about to take."

"I don't think the risks are that big," Gray said.

"From what I can see, Lattimer Spices is ready for the expansion. You're well capitalized. You've already got exposure via your catalogues."

"That's right. But we're not on every shelf in America, and that's where we want to be."

Gray leaned forward as he jumped in with both feet and gave his spiel. No time like the present to wow the boss with his ideas. Lattimer kept nodding, which Gray took as a good sign. He interrupted a few times, but only for questions or clarification.

"Excuse me, gentlemen."

Gray looked up at Shelby's voice, then he checked his watch. He'd been talking for almost thirty minutes.

"I thought you might want something to eat while you talk. And perhaps some nice cold tea."

Lattimer stood, and Gray followed suit. Shelby came around the couch carrying a large tray of food, which surprised him. The fridge had been less than bountiful, so where had this all come from?

She set the tray down, then handed each of them a napkin. "Please, help yourself. Mr. Lattimer, how do you like your tea?"

"It's Jim, ma'am."

She smiled that kind smile. "Shelby."

He took a cracker from the tray. It had something on top, but Gray couldn't tell what. "I like my tea sweet, just like my women."

Shelby laughed and handed him a glass. "Now, how come I already guessed that?"

He sipped the tea. "It's perfect."

"Ah, you're just trying to flatter me."

"Flattering you is easy." He drank again, nearly finishing the tall glass, but Shelby was ready with a pitcher. Lattimer popped the cracker in his mouth. As he chewed, his eyes widened, and Gray's heart stopped beating.

The big man swallowed. "What was that?"

"Did you like it?" Shelby asked.

"Heck, yes, I liked it."

"Good, because I made it with your mesquite rub."

"No."

She nodded. "Everything on the tray has been made with Lattimer spices."

He smiled, took a few more items from the tray, then sat on the couch. He ate a little sandwich, then slapped his knee. "Peanut butter, jelly and jalapeño?"

"Right."

"Delicious." He turned to Gray. "Go on. Try some."

Gray tried one of the crackers. It was good. Really good. Different. He looked at Shelby. She was smiling contentedly, and he wondered if she realized what she'd done. He'd never have thought of this. Even if he'd known Lattimer planned to stop by.

"It's too quiet," she said. "I think I'd better go check on the twins."

"Thanks," he whispered as she walked by. The next second, her cheeks were bright pink. He liked that. He liked that a lot.

"Hell of a nice surprise," Lattimer said as he folded his napkin and put it on the tray. "Now I'm not at all sorry your phone wasn't working."

"About that," Gray said. "The kids. They were playing hide and seek with all the telephones."

"Don't worry about it. I've got kids of my own.

They're grown now, but my oldest, Darlene, she's expecting.''

"Congratulations."

He smiled as he leaned back. "My first grandchild. Of course Betty, she's my wife, is jumping out of her boots. She's buying every baby doodad from here to New York. She's going to spoil the child something awful."

"I have the feeling she won't be the only one."

He laughed. "You got it. I tell you, Gray, kids are everything. My family means more to me than all the money in the world."

Gray nodded as if he felt the same way.

"There's nothing that makes more of a difference in a man's life." He stared at the box of Lincoln Logs on the floor, his gaze fixed. Then he shook himself out of his reverie, slapped his knee and stood up. "I'd better let you get back to your day."

Gray stood, too. "It's been a real pleasure meeting you, sir."

"The pleasure was mine."

They walked to the front door, and Lattimer stepped outside. "You thank that pretty lady for the wonderful food."

"I will."

Lattimer extended his hand. "Tell you what. Why don't you and the missus come on over to my place on Saturday night? My secretary will call you with the details. If you find your phones, that is."

Gray shook his head. "Shelby—"

The big man's cell phone rang, and Lattimer whipped it off his belt like a six-shooter. "Lattimer."

Gray waited for him to get off the phone. But from the look on Lattimer's face, he got the feeling it would be a while. Then Jim waved and pointed to his phone. He was leaving—before Gray had a chance to tell him that Shelby wasn't the missus.

Sure enough, Lattimer turned and headed toward his car without another look back.

Gray watched him climb into his Cadillac and drive away. When the car had disappeared down the road, Gray relaxed his shoulders. It had gone well. Except for that little misunderstanding.

It hadn't occurred to Gray that Lattimer would think Shelby was his wife. He probably thought the twins were his, too. Clearly Lattimer felt strongly about family. Very strongly. It was even possible that once he found out Gray was single, the job might not be in the pocket.

He closed the front door, going over their conversation. He really felt he'd done well. The job was his. He knew it. It didn't matter if he was married or not. In fact, it was probably better that he wasn't married. He'd have more time to devote to the company.

Still, with guys like Lattimer, who knew what little quirk could tip the scale? Maybe it wasn't a bad thing if he believed Shelby was the missus for a while. What could it hurt?

CHAPTER FIVE

"'No, MISS PIGGY. I haven't found your earrings. If I had found them, I would have given them to you.'" Shelby looked up from the book she was reading and glanced at the clock. It was almost two. Late for a nap, but with Lattimer's surprise visit... Then she checked on the twins. Scout was out, and Jem was moments away. He was struggling, though. His eyes would close, jerk open, then drift closed again. Another page, and it would be all over but the sweet dreams.

"'But what am I supposed to do?' Miss Piggy asked. 'I can't go back home without them.'" She heard a footfall. It was Gray. He tiptoed into the room.

"Are you almost finished?" he whispered.

She nodded. "About two more minutes."

"I'll meet you downstairs." He walked out again, and her gaze lingered on the door for a long moment after he was gone.

She'd done well today. She'd helped him with the children. She'd helped him with his job. All in all, she had every reason to feel content. Yet...

She'd never been more aware of her own patterns. Not that she was a psychologist or anything, but she'd read her fair share of self-help books. The thing she did best in all the world was come to the rescue. She was the cavalry, riding in to save the fort. The Saint Bernard after the avalanche. It was all well and good, except for her motives. She'd changed after her long stay in the hospital. She'd become a follower instead of a leader, and she'd let the other children walk all over her. She was just so grateful anyone liked her at all.

She'd gotten better, of course. No way she'd let anyone take advantage of her now, but there was still this need inside her to help. To fix. To meddle. To mend. To be liked. Needed.

She glanced over the top of the book. Jem had lost the battle to stay awake. She put the book on the dresser, made sure both kids were covered by their comforters and then left them.

Gray wasn't in the living room. She picked up the almost empty tray and pushed through the swinging doors to the kitchen. He was sitting at the table, with the phone he'd repaired and an open bottle of beer. He tapped the phone. "It works."

"Congratulations."

He smiled, then nodded in the general direction of upstairs. "They asleep?"

"Sound asleep."

"Come on and sit down. Want a beer?"

She shook her head. "I'm not much of a beer drinker."

He gave her a half smile. "I guessed that. I figure you're more of a white wine kind of gal."

"White wine?"

"Or tea. I bet you drink lots of tea."

"Now, what makes you say that?" She sat across from him and waited for his explanation.

"Tea is what you drink with friends. I bet you have lots of those, too."

"I do. But we rarely have tea."

"I'm not talking about that kind of tea. I mean iced tea, like you served Lattimer. Big pitchers. With tall glasses that are somehow always full."

"Okay. I'll give you that."

"I knew it."

"How?"

"The way you stepped in with the big guy. How easy and natural it was for you."

"I was just being hospitable."

"Exactly. I bet that restaurant of yours does a hell of a business." He leaned forward and put both arms on the table. "And I bet everyone orders twice as much when you're cooking."

"Oh, I'm not the chef."

"What?"

"I'm not."

"Huh. I don't figure."

She shrugged. "Don't get me wrong, I love to cook. But I have too many other things to do at the restaurant to be the chef. Although I do step in from time to time."

He looked at her through narrowed eyes. "I think I'd like to be there when you stepped in."

"If you're trying to flatter me into staying, it won't work."

He sat back as if she'd surprised him. "I wasn't trying any such thing."

"Are you sure?" she asked, mirroring his stance of a moment ago.

He sighed. Looked at the table. Then at her. "All

right, so the thought had crossed my mind. But every word I said is true.''

''Right.''

''Have I ever lied to you before?''

''I have no idea.''

He smiled easily and took a generous swig of beer. ''You know what doesn't make sense?''

She shook her head.

''That you're not married.''

''Why, because I know how to make finger sandwiches?''

''No. Because you're the kind of woman any man with half a brain would want for a wife.''

''I beg your pardon?''

''I don't mean it as an insult. I know it's not politically correct, but I can't help what I know. You take care of things that most men don't have a clue about. Remember what this place looked like when you got here? You handle things. Make it all manageable.''

She almost denied it. But it was just what she'd been thinking upstairs. ''You know what, Gray Jackson? You're right.''

''I am?''

''Don't look so damned pleased with yourself. It was a lucky guess.''

''Lucky guess?'' He raised a disdainful brow. ''I happen to be incredibly intuitive.''

''Oh, really?''

He nodded. ''It's a gift. I can't take all the credit for it. Some people are just born this way.''

''Oh, please.'' She got up and opened the fridge, secretly tickled with the teasing tone of the conversation, if not the subject matter. She got one of the kids' juice boxes and struggled for a minute to get the straw in it. Then she sat down again. "All right. I've got a little observation of my own."

"Shoot."

"You have never had a relationship that lasted more than five months."

He kept a completely straight face. But then he nodded. Just once. "And you know this…"

"I know this because I, too, am an acute observer of the human condition."

"Yeah, you are cute, but that doesn't answer my question."

"Very funny."

He nodded. "Come on. You're not getting out of this."

She took a long sip of fruit punch and nearly gagged at the sweetness. "Hold that thought," she said. Then she got a glass, poured in the drink and added some club soda from the pantry. When she glanced at Gray, his gaze was on her. It was such an unguarded look—not sad so much as resigned.

By the time she sat down again, he'd snapped out of it. His cocky attitude was back, and so was his charm. "The seconds are ticking by, Shelby. You only have two lifelines left."

"Yeah? I'll ask the audience."

"Sorry. This time the audience has asked you."

"Let's see. How did I know you never had a relationship that lasted more than a few months? First, you're gorgeous and you know it."

He nearly spit the beer he'd been drinking. From the way he coughed, she thought some might have gone up his nose. "You okay?"

He lurched to the sink and got a paper towel, and after wiping his face, he wiped the table. "I'm fine."

"Shall I go on?"

"I'm not sure."

"You've gotten away with murder for most of your life. People forgive you. All the time. For some really awful things."

He didn't say anything. Or look at her.

"You test people. You like to see how much you can get away with. Am I close?"

He nodded slowly.

"But when you win, it doesn't feel like a victory. It's kind of awful, isn't it?"

He forced a smile. "Is it too late to change the subject?"

"No. You can change it right now. It's okay."

He didn't say anything for a long while. He drank his beer. Stared at his hands. "I stole a magazine once. When I was about eight. *Rolling Stone,* of all things. I stole it, and the manager caught me. But I was standing by this girl. Her name was Heidi and she was in my class. We weren't friends. I'd hardly ever spoken to her. But she marched right up to the manager and said she'd tricked me. She said she'd told me she'd paid for the magazine, but that she didn't want her mother to see. It was her fault."

"And I suppose he believed her?"

"Why wouldn't he?"

"Right. So what happened? With Heidi, I mean?"

"To the best of my recollection, I was mean to her for the rest of the school year. Not brutally. I didn't hurt her or anything. But I ignored her."

"Which was probably worse."

"Yeah. She was a nice girl. Lots of freckles."

"Funny how the patterns start so early."

"Makes me wonder if they're hard-wired."

She drank some of her doctored brew. It was fine now—not too sweet. "I think they are. But that doesn't mean we can't change."

"That's a contradiction."

"No, it isn't. We still have choices to make."

"I don't know a lot of people who've changed. Do you?"

"As a matter of fact, I do. I have some very good friends who have changed some fundamentally hard stuff. And they did it in a very short time."

"How?"

"The motivation was really strong. Which, I think, is the key."

"What, they were going be hung at dawn?"

She laughed. "No. They were faced with losing the person they loved."

"Love? You're telling me love is the answer?"

"Yes."

"Oh, God, you *do* need a husband."

"You don't believe in love?"

"I didn't say that. I just don't think it changes people. I think that's a myth. Like the Easter bunny or store-bought pizza that's supposed to taste like it was delivered."

"I do. I think there are only a few things that can change people. For one thing, I think a spiritual experience can alter everything."

"Okay, I'll give you that one. Next?"

Her gaze moved to her hands. To the clear, smooth skin there. "Accidents can change a person. You know, falling off a horse and becoming a paraplegic.

Losing a limb.'' She raised her gaze to meet his. ''Fire. A fire can change everything.''

He nodded slowly, and she waited for a comment, but all he said was, ''Okay. So I'll give you that one, too.''

''And last, but certainly not least, is love. I think love can turn a world upside down.''

''Well, Shelby,'' he said. ''You're wrong about this one.''

''Subtle.''

He cocked a brow. ''I know a guy. John is his name. John has a little problem with betting on the ponies. John met someone. Her name was Marsha. He was crazy about Marsha and vice versa. He swore up and down and sideways that now that he was going to be with Marsha, he would never bet on the ponies again. Want to guess the outcome?''

''He gambled away their wedding money.''

''Close. They didn't get that far. She left him right after the engagement.''

''But that's an addiction.''

''So addictions are stronger than love?''

''Hmm. I'm not sure. But I don't think so.''

''Even after my stunningly poignant example?''

''Sorry.''

''You're just a hopeless romantic.''

She nodded. ''True. Not that there's anyone in my life to be a romantic about.''

''No? That doesn't make much sense. You should be dating.''

''It's not that simple.''

''Shelby, you're a nice gal. You're a great cook, and you're the best damn Samaritan in all of Texas, but you're a dope.''

''Thanks.''

''You're welcome.''

''You're not going to expand on that?''

''No. At least not right this second.''

''All right,'' she said, giving in none too graciously. ''How long have the kids been asleep?''

He shook his head, then got up. ''I'll go check on them.''

She watched him leave the room, and while she still admired the body, she felt just a bit wiser about the man. He was as much trouble as a man could be. The kind of guy who loves 'em and leaves 'em and doesn't even know he was a tornado in their lives. She didn't believe he was malicious. Not at all. Just clueless. Because life, for a man like Gray, was very, very different than it was for a woman like her.

He'd get his job. And he'd do spectacularly well. Until he got bored. Then he'd move on. Simple. But it was sadly selfish.

They were opposites, she and Gray. She gave too much. He gave too little. Between them, they'd probably make a terrific person.

He came back a few minutes later. ''They're both sound asleep,'' he said as he took his seat.

''The calm before the storm.''

''Yeah.''

''May I ask you a question?''

''It's too late to be shy,'' he said with a wry smile.

''Right. Why on earth did you agree to take care of the twins?''

''It's complicated.''

''Okay.''

He looked her up and down, then shook his head.

''What?''

"I don't know. I just find it hard to believe I only met you yesterday."

"Why?"

"Because you know too damn much for my own good."

"Thanks."

"That wasn't a compliment."

She smiled. "Yes, it was. You think I'm perceptive. Wise beyond my years."

"And modest, too."

"Look who's talking."

"Touché."

"So answer me."

"My sister-in-law had to go to Dallas for some tests. Their regular sitter is out of town. Ipso facto, here I am."

"And?"

"And we agreed that there would be day sitters from the agency to do the real work. I was enlisted in a supervisory capacity."

"Uh-oh."

"And I believe that's where you stepped in."

"When are they coming back?"

"In a couple of days. If things go well."

"Ah."

He looked at her. Looked away. She could see he was dying to ask her to stay. But that wouldn't be very smart of her, would it? "The problem is," she said, not bothering to wait for him to ask her, "if I stay, I'm just perpetuating behavior that I'm trying to change."

"Right. And if I get you to stay, I'm just using my manipulative skills to get what I want."

"So we're agreed, then?"

"Oh, yeah. You have to leave. In fact, I'm getting ready to throw you out."

"Very good. I think that's wise."

"Right."

"But what are you going to give the twins for dinner?"

His brow furrowed. Even that made him look sexy. "I do believe they have a McDonald's in this neck of the woods."

"Ah, excellent choice."

"You see? I'm not totally helpless."

"Of course not."

"I figure I'm a lot bigger than they are, right?"

"Right."

"And they're only two kids, right?"

"Right."

"So we'll get through it."

"Absolutely."

He nodded several times, more to himself than at her. He got up, took his beer to the sink. He looked outside for a few seconds, then nodded again. Finally, he turned and came back to the table. He came right up to where she was sitting. He took her hand in his. "Shelby?"

"Yes?"

He suddenly dropped to one knee. "Please stay. Please, please, please. I'm begging. I need you. They're going to wake up soon, and all hell will break loose. There's dinner. And bedtime. And oh, God, the rest is too frightening to contemplate."

She burst out laughing. "You wimp."

"Yes, yes. I'm a wimp of the first order. So you must help me. And do it soon, because I'm going to realize any second that I'm on my friggin' knees in the kitchen, and then I'll have nightmares for weeks.''

''Oh, you poor psychologically wounded puppy.''

''Yes. I am. I'm a textbook case of the Peter Pan principle. But that doesn't mean I don't really need your help.''

She shook her head, knowing if she opened her mouth she'd be in serious trouble.

''Okay, okay. No problem. You don't have to stay. I can handle it.'' He stood, wiped his hands as if it was a done deal. But the look in his eyes wasn't quite so certain.

She should say no. She should let him stand on his own two feet. Let him rise to the challenge. But then, wasn't that just another form of her fixing everyone?

Staying was out of the question. Absolutely. She'd already half fallen in love with the guy, and if she stayed, she'd be in serious trouble.

His eyes were filled with so much doubt. And they were such nice eyes. Such long lashes. Oh, Lord, he was too adorable for words. She *couldn't* stay.

Then the son of a gun really turned the screws. His cocky smile faltered. Just for a moment. Knowing better, she felt her resolve slip away. She'd regret it, but she was going to stay. God, she was a such a sap. ''Just until dinner. Then I'm out of here.''

He grabbed her hands and pulled her to her feet. She fell into his arms, and a second later his lips were on hers, and oh, my God...

CHAPTER SIX

THE PLEASURE of her warm, soft lips hit him gradually. He hadn't meant to kiss her. And he sure as hell hadn't meant to like it so much. But as long as he was here…

He closed his eyes as he stepped closer, still holding her, drinking in her scent and then, unable to help himself, tasting her. Instead of the sound thrashing he expected, her lips parted. Not much. Just enough for him to slip inside.

He heard her sharp intake of breath, felt the air stir and an immediate tightening of his chest and all points south. Her tongue touched his. A jolt hit him so hard he jerked back, as if she was a live wire.

She stood very still. Her lips still parted. Her eyes fixed and glassy. The color of her cheeks reminded him of pink roses.

What he wanted to know was what the hell had just happened? His innocent little thank-you kiss had turned around and whopped him upside the head.

It was much worse than he'd anticipated. A hell of a lot worse. Sure, she was nice and sexy, but he usually went for long, tall, somewhat vacuous women who spent the better part of the day deciding on a pair of shoes. Who would never make him think about children, or even a future past the weekend.

Shelby came back from wherever she'd been. She

focused on him with utter surprise. No, more like shock.

So she hadn't expected it, either. The pink on her cheeks turned to red and spread down her neck to her chest. She cleared her throat, then looked at him questioningly. "What would you have done if I'd agreed to stay for the weekend?"

He laughed, and that's all it took to chase away the weirdness of the moment. "I don't think you want to know."

"I—"

Just then a high-pitched cry came from the other end of the house.

"Scout," Shelby said. "I'd better—"

"No. Let me. I'll holler if we need you."

"Are you sure?"

"I'm sure." The whole way to the kids' room, he thought about what had just happened. Normally, he knew when he was going to kiss someone. He knew what kind of a kiss it was going to be. And he knew the effect he wanted to achieve by said kiss. To the best of his knowledge, none of his criteria had been met.

So what was the deal? And, a much more important question, what should he do about it? His first thought was simple—nothing. She was leaving in a few hours. End of story.

Or was it?

Even the prospect of finding out why Scout was yelling her head off couldn't mask the fact that he didn't want Shelby to go. Which was a hell of a thing.

As he reached the bedroom, he heard a very strident young lady cry, "It's my turn!"

He pushed open the door, expecting pandemonium.

He remembered what it was like when he was a little kid. He and Ben used to fight all the time. Hitting, spitting, kicking. It was all fair game. But neither of them wanted to fight with Kate. She was devious. She hit below the belt. And she almost always won. That is, until they reached puberty, and he and Ben each grew a foot taller than her. But even then, she was a wily opponent.

He'd learned to respect women from watching her. And, truth be known, to fear them a little bit. They just came up with such bizarre stuff! Half the time he didn't know what the hell women were talking about. He'd learned early to stop trying to figure them out.

As if to prove his point, Scout punched Jem right in the stomach, then *she* burst out crying. "He won't give me the blue dinosaur!"

At least that's what he thought she said. Her voice was wobbly and full of hiccups. "Why not?"

"I don't *know!*"

"He's mine. She can't have him 'cause he's mine!"

"Do you have another one?"

Jem shook his head, all the while glaring murderously at his sister. "They're *all* mine!"

"It's not fair!"

"It is so!"

"You boogerhead!"

"Poopoo pants!"

"Baby!"

"Caca nose!"

"Hold it!"

The kids stopped. They'd never heard Uncle Gray lose it before. "You, Jem. Give me the dinosaur."

"But—" The little boy didn't go on. He handed over the blue stuffed toy.

"No one gets to play with any dinosaurs. In fact, we are now declaring this a dinosaur-free zone. No exceptions. Is that clear?"

Scout sniffed.

Jem wiped his nose with his arm.

"Good enough," Gray said. "Now come on downstairs. Both of you."

As they walked out of the room, Gray put his hand on Jem's shoulder. "Listen up, Jem, old man. I've got something to tell you."

"What?" he said, his voice as unhappy as a four-year-old's could be.

"This isn't the last time you're going to have to give up your dinosaur."

"Why not?"

"Because we share the planet with women."

"We do?"

Gray stopped at the top of the staircase. So did Jem. They watched Scout climb to the bottom, then head for the kitchen. When she was out of earshot, Gray sat and put Jem a step down, facing him. "Yes, we do. The thing to remember is that you're never going to understand them. Ever. You'll think you do, but— ha, ha!—that's what they want you to think."

"Huh?"

"Oh, it gets worse. They're the ones with the *real* blue dinosaur, and they won't let us have it until we jump through hoops. You have to buy them dinners and flowers and take them to parties. You have to listen to them talk about clothes and hair products. God forbid you don't drive the right car, though. Yeah, right. They won't let you forget that."

"Forget what?"

"And then there's the whole jewelry thing. Once you go there, it's all over."

"Huh?"

Gray caught sight of Jem's face. He was completely confused and maybe just a little scared. "Never mind."

"Okay."

"Go on down and find Shelby. Tell her what you want for dinner."

Jem nodded, turned and made his way down the stairs. Gray was still thinking about all the blue dinosaurs he'd wanted to play with. He got up, headed for the kitchen. Shelby. Shelby with the red hair. And those lips. Maybe he could get her to stay for the night. Just for kicks. No big deal. He would get her to stay, they'd have a nice time in the sack, and just like always, he'd say goodbye without a backward glance. That would chase away all this crap about kids and marriage. Hell, it would be good for both of them. Damn near therapeutic.

He looked at the toy in his hand and smiled.

SHELBY'S GAZE was on the backyard herb garden, but her thoughts were on Gray. On the feel of his lips on hers. How long had it been since she'd been kissed? Really kissed? God, years. She hadn't felt the lack until now. The last time was anything but a pleasant memory. She'd been twenty-one, still in college. She'd met him at a party after too many beers. He'd seduced her in a way that had made her reckless, daring. They'd gone to her place. The lights had been off, so it was safe. But they hadn't stayed off.

He'd seen her back, and a moment later he'd remembered something he had to do. At two in the morning.

But Gray had kissed her after he'd seen her. Seen part of her, at least. But he knew the extent of the scarring. And he'd still kissed her.

The temptation to indulge her fantasies was strong. To imagine him kissing her again. To picture him in her bed. Her body ached for his touch, it had been without for so long. But it was only a kiss. Not a prelude to seduction.

She hugged herself, her T-shirt no barrier to the cool November air. It was time to leave. Time to end the charade and go home to her life. To her very singular life.

The thing was, she didn't want to leave, even though she knew she was walking on very thin ice. That she could fall through any moment, and there would be no rescue.

But he'd kissed her after *he'd seen the scars.*

What if…?

She closed her eyes and forced herself to think logically. Gray was an incredibly good-looking man. Charming, well-educated, funny, sexy. He was meant for the supermodels of the world, not the Shelby Lords. The only reason on earth he was paying any attention to her was that she'd come to him at a time he needed help. If they'd met at a party, he'd have looked right through her. No way she would have been in the running.

So why did she think there could be anything between them now? One kiss did not a relationship make.

On the other hand, what if this wasn't about a relationship at all? What if it was about something far more basic?

She was almost twenty-six—a long enough time to be a virgin. Too long. He had a real clear idea what she looked like, and he'd kissed her anyway. Maybe he'd want to do more. This time, the lights would stay off. This time, he had nowhere to go.

A shiver hit her, but not from the cold. It was fear. Fear and hope and longing all wrapped together in a sharp bundle. It made sense to do it here. To do it with a man she'd never see again. If she was humiliated, at least it wouldn't be on her home turf.

Of course, it was all predicated on Gray. On whether he wanted her.

The thought, him wanting her, felt utterly outrageous. But she didn't want to close off the possibility before she knew. If it was no, then she'd leave. But if it was yes...

She should have brought better underwear.

GRAY PLUCKED more napkins from the silver dispenser on the counter, then took the food-laden tray to the far table where Jem, Scout and Shelby waited. He heard their laughter, and it made him smile, not even knowing what the joke was. They looked like a family. Scout standing on the seat. Jem playing with a salt packet. Shelby keeping a keen, gentle eye on them.

He would ask her to stay as soon as they got home. Make it seem inevitable. It would be after dark. She shouldn't drive alone at night. His stomach tightened. It occurred to him that he hadn't felt that particular brand of nervousness in years. It felt...interesting.

Jem waved him over. "Hurry, Uncle Gray. I'm starving."

"Yeah, just withering away from hunger," he said as he put the tray on the table. Shelby gave the kids their meals and sodas, then took her burger and fries. He sat next to her, and for the next half hour he played Ozzie to her Harriet. He had to open ketchup packages, wipe up spills, get Jem to eat his food instead of play with it. They were the epitome of domestication, and he was actually having a good time.

He wasn't afraid of the kids any longer. He wouldn't go so far as to say he would know what to do in an emergency, but he could now bathe them, feed them, put them to bed. It wasn't that hard, either.

"What is that smug smile about?"

He hadn't realized his satisfaction had been so obvious. He turned to Shelby, who had a dot of ketchup on her lower lip. "Smug? Me?" He shook his head. "Nah." Then he wiped the ketchup off with his thumb.

Her startled gaze met his. Her tongue darted out to moisten her lips. To touch the spot he'd just touched.

Within seconds, he went from Ozzie to Don Juan. In that nothing little moment, everything had shifted. During the trip to McDonald's he'd pretty much talked himself out of seducing her for the hell of it. Suddenly it seemed stupid not to. It didn't help to remind himself she wasn't his type. Maybe he needed to amend that. She was *also* his type.

He doubted very much anyone would believe him—he hardly believed it himself—but he actually was attracted to a woman more for what she was like on the inside than the outside. Not that the outside wasn't nice, but that wasn't the prime motivating force here. He liked being near her. He wanted to see what she would be like in bed.

"You know what I was thinking?" he asked.

"About the repercussions of the free trade market?"

He gave her a look that told her to knock it off. "I was thinking about tonight."

"What about it?"

"I think you should stay the night."

"You do?"

He nodded as he watched her cheeks turn pink. "I do. It's going to be eight by the time we get home. Nine by the time we get the kids down, and by then it's too late for you to be out driving."

"It is?"

He nodded. "Anything could happen to you out there. Stay the night, and leave in the morning. If you want to." Without waiting for her answer he turned to Jem and Scout. "Right, kids?"

Their deafening yes made half the restaurant stare.

"The verdict is in and it's unanimous. You need to stay."

Her smile fell as she studied him for a long moment. He wondered what she was looking for and if she found it. What did she think of him? Did she know he wasn't usually like this? That he was walking in unfamiliar territory?

Of course she did. That was the thing. She knew who he was. Had known from moment one. Crazy.

"All right."

"Pardon?"

"I said all right. I'll stay."

He grinned, pleased with his victory. "Great."

"But only on one condition."

"Uh-oh."

"I want you to tell me why I should."

"Huh?"

She looked away for a moment, then met his gaze. "Why do you want me to stay? Is it to help with the children?"

Her voice had gotten softer, just above a whisper. He glanced at the kids. They were playing with their toys, not paying any attention to the action on this side of the booth. Facing Shelby again wasn't so easy. She expected the truth from him. Should he tell it?

"Well?"

"It's partly because of the kids."

"What's the other part?"

"I want you to stay."

"Why?"

"You aren't making this easy."

She nodded. "Why?"

"Because I like you."

"Like? As in buddies, pals? Or like, as in you were thinking of kissing me again?"

He felt his face heat, but he didn't weasel out. He kept his gaze locked on hers. His peripheral vision caught something, though, and he looked at her mouth. Her lower lip—the one he'd touched—quivered. She was scared out of her mind. Damn, that was tricky. Maybe not. All he had to do was tell her the truth. "While I'd like to think we are potential buddies, I was also thinking about kissing you again."

"Oh," she said, but it wasn't a word so much as a sigh. Her eyes closed for a moment, and when she opened them again they were tellingly shiny.

"My turn," he said. "Were you thinking of kissing me back?"

She nodded once. "I think."

"What does that mean?"

Her gaze left his. She stared at her diet cola. "I'm not very good at this kind of thing."

"I've already kissed you, remember? I had no complaints."

"I—"

The moment between him and Shelby ended when Jem knocked his soda to the floor. Or at least it was put on hold. Gray wanted the kids to hurry up and eat. He fully intended to pursue the matter the moment they were alone.

Shelby took another bite of her burger, but she didn't taste a thing. What was important here was not to panic. Not to run screaming from the room. She'd asked. He'd answered.

Up to the very last second, she'd been prepared for disappointment. In fact, she didn't know what to do now, because she'd never seriously entertained the notion that he would really, really want to…

She put down the burger. Was she honestly going to go through with this? With *him?* He must have been with dozens of women, all of them beautiful, talented and experienced. What did he want with a scarred virgin from Austin?

Stop it, she commanded herself. Why didn't she deserve this? Why couldn't it be her turn?

Her gaze went to Gray, who'd finished mopping up Jem's spill. To the right of their booth, a woman walked past, but not so quickly that she didn't have time to give Gray a dazzling smile. The woman didn't seem to mind that he was with Shelby and the kids. Her eyes held a blatant invitation. In addition to her colossal chutzpah, she also had legs that went up to her neck and boobs that could take an eye out. She was gorgeous, and she knew it.

Shelby couldn't see Gray's expression, but she did see his shoulders straighten, his hand flex into a fist. She saw that he didn't turn away from the woman. On the contrary, he followed her with his eyes as she crossed the room and found her table. Several long seconds later, Gray's eyes came back to her.

"So, we almost through here?"

"I'm through," she said.

His brows lowered instantly. "What's wrong?"

"Nothing."

"Are you sure?"

She nodded. She didn't want anything to be wrong. She wanted to believe. So badly. She put her trash on the tray, then turned to the kids. "Let's go home."

GRAY DIDN'T touch her once on the way home. Not once. Not even a casual brush of his hand. And when they got home and got the kids into pajamas, he seemed distant, changed.

She shouldn't have agreed to stay. In fact, she wouldn't stay. She'd finish cleaning up the kitchen and leave. It had been a stupid dream, one that could never come true. The confusing part was that she'd seen something in his eyes. When he'd asked her to stay she'd been looking right at him, and she could have sworn she saw hunger there. Hunger and want and desire. She knew, because she'd seen that look before. Only before, when she'd seen that look, the hunger had been for some other woman. Never for her.

She'd seen it with Mitchell Maitland when he talked about his wife, Darcy Taylor. She'd seen it in her brother's eyes, when Michael finally realized he loved Jenny.

In the wee hours, when she confessed her deepest desires, she'd wished for a man to look at her like that. Like Gray had looked at her.

"Shelby?"

He startled her. She'd been so deep in thought she hadn't heard him enter the kitchen. "Yes?"

"I've had a great day today. In fact, I don't think I've ever met anyone easier to talk to."

"Come on, Gray. You know that's not true."

He took hold of her arm and turned her toward him. "It is true. I think you know that. I'm not sure what, but something is happening here. Between us. I can feel it, and I know you feel it, too. At least, you did about two hours ago."

She opened her mouth to say…what? She had no idea. But she could see he was waiting for her to speak. "Where are the kids?"

Frustration changed his expression. She could see he wanted to throttle her, which was pretty damn cool all by itself.

"Watching a movie, and don't change the subject."

This was it. The moment that would decide her fate. Or at the very least, where she was going to sleep tonight. What if she just went for it? What was the worst thing that could happen? So sparks wouldn't fly. The angels wouldn't sing. So what? She'd been disappointed before and lived through it. What she hadn't done before, ever, was take the initiative. Go after what she wanted. And what had all this waiting gotten her? Zip. *Nada*. Besides, if it all went to hell, she'd never see him again. She took a deep breath and dove in headfirst. "All right. I agree. Something is happening here. So what are we going to do about it?"

Gray leaned forward as he pulled her closer. "Let me show you."

CHAPTER SEVEN

SHELBY LIFTED her face, parted her lips, then closed her eyes. She was ready for the bells and whistles.

Gray wanted nothing more than to kiss the woman senseless. But something held him back. He didn't want to hurt her, not for anything. As strong as she was in most areas, there was real vulnerability here. He had the feeling she'd been hurt before. That somewhere along the way some idiot had said something or done something....

On the other hand, if he backed away now, who knew what she'd think. He didn't want to embarrass her, either. She'd been terrific, and damn it, he wanted her to stay. But—

Her eyes opened. Her right brow lifted, and she shook her head in a very small move. The next thing he knew, she was on tiptoes, her arms went around his neck, and then *she* kissed *him*.

It was a hell of a surprise. A nice surprise. He still didn't understand what was going on between them, but at the moment, he didn't care. All he knew for sure was that her lips were soft and welcoming. Her scent did strange things to his insides. And the way she tasted, the way her hot tongue felt on his was enough to make the rest of the world fade away.

He encircled her with his arms, pulling her tight against him. Her breasts flattened against his chest, but not so much that he couldn't feel her hard nipples. He touched her back. She flinched, but she didn't try to stop him. Which was a good thing, because he didn't think he could stop. He ran his hands down her back to her lush bottom, and even though he hardly touched her there, he became instantly, painfully aroused.

She moved her hips and nipped his lower lip. He moaned, wanting to take her right this second, right on the kitchen table. It was crazy. He'd never felt this strong a pull before. Not even at seventeen. This was off the scale, and damn it, if he didn't do something about it soon, he'd embarrass himself, which wasn't a smart way to impress a woman.

He moved against her, letting her feel what she was doing to him. Her tongue thrust boldly in his mouth, and he guided her toward the table.

"Can I have ice cream?"

Shelby jerked out of his arms, leaving him with his mouth open and his libido in full throttle. He turned to the sink and plunged his hands in the water while Shelby went over to Jem.

"You want ice cream?" she asked, her voice strained and breathy.

"Yes. Scout does, too. But she had to go potty."

"Oh. Okay. Well, then, let's see." Shelby opened the refrigerator, closed it, then opened the freezer. "Ice cream, ice cream, ice cream—there it is." She pulled out a half-gallon tub of Blue Bell vanilla.

Gray focused on the dishes while he tried to make some sense out of his predicament. It was his reaction to her that had him wondering if he'd been hypnotized or something. Ever since she'd walked into the living room this morning, things had been off. Not off in a bad way, but there was no mistaking how off they were.

He'd told her things he'd never meant to say.

He'd let Lattimer think she was his wife.

He'd almost made love to her on his brother's kitchen table.

It was nuts. Or maybe he was nuts.

He washed the plates from lunch while she brought out two bowls for the kids. Scout clambered in, a plastic telephone bouncing on the floor behind her. She told Shelby that there was a phone call for her. Without missing a beat, Shelby put the phone to her ear and had a lively conversation with nobody, sending Scout into a fit of giggles. What a sound.

He finished the dishes. He washed the silverware, purposefully taking it nice and slow. Watching Shelby entertain his niece had, for some bizarre reason, brought back the obsession to send the kids to bed and continue where he and Shelby had left off.

As if his thoughts had spurred Jem, the little boy's spoon clattered in his empty dish, then he darted out of the room. "Donkey Kong!"

Scout's eyes widened, and she quickly gulped a spoonful of vanilla ice cream, then she, too, darted off, leaving her telephone on the floor beside her chair.

Shelby bent to pick it up, but from the wrong angle. He couldn't see anything good. Damn it, what was he doing! And why did he care so much? Since when did he start having a conscience? He turned to the sink and started scrubbing a pot for all he was worth.

Shelby walked over with the ice cream paraphernalia. He didn't even look at her. But then she walked past him. Real close. Her arm brushed against his, causing havoc throughout his entire body. When he looked at her, she was leaning against the kitchen door. Her smile was hesitant, but her eyes were full of questions.

He left the pot, wiped his hands on a dish towel, then headed for the redhead who had stolen his good sense. He caught her gaze—held it steady. Then got real close to her. He put his hand on the wall behind her head, which made him lean in until they were inches apart. He could feel her heat. Smell her womanly scent. See the battle in her eyes as she went from brazen to frightened then back again.

He lowered his head, and she gasped seconds before his lips met hers. He took his sweet time, tasting her, teasing her. He didn't touch her. All he did was kiss her the way she wanted to be kissed. He knew the fight was over when her hand went to his chest. She was his. And he wouldn't disappoint her.

She pulled away. "We have to put the children to bed."

He nodded. "And then?"

Her gaze shifted from him to the kitchen door. "I don't know."

"Sure you do."

"No, I don't."

He smiled. She may not want to admit it, but she'd already made up her mind. He'd let her bring it up, though. Let her make the first move.

"MARY JANE, please pick up. It's me, and I need help."

Shelby waited impatiently for her friend to answer

her phone. Nothing. "Mary Jane, don't do this to me! You have to be there."

More nothing. She closed her eyes and drank in some much-needed air. "I'm in Blue Point," she said, giving Mary Jane the phone number. "It's a dead end as far as my birth mother goes, but oh, God, Mary Jane, I think I'm going to do something really reckless. Or brave. I'm not sure which. There's this guy here. His name is Gray."

Shelby's gaze went to the bathroom door, checking once again that it was locked. It was. She had her privacy. The only thing she didn't have was a clue about what to do next. "He's gorgeous. And he kissed me. But then I kissed him! Can you stand it? I'm helping him take care of his niece and nephew, and I'm spending the night. But I don't know what to do about the whole, uh, bed thing. I know I can sleep with him, and damn it, why not? I'm a full-grown woman. On the other hand—"

The beep signaled the end of the tape on Mary Jane's machine. Shelby thought about calling back, but that seemed a bit much. She could call Lana. But it was late, and her sister would probably think she was crazy. There was Abby. Or Anna. Or...

Nobody. How about if she made this decision all by her lonesome? How about if she tried listening to her own instincts? How about if she let her heart lead for once?

It wasn't as if she were deciding whether or not to marry the guy. This was one night. Either way, she was determined not to have any regrets. So she could march right into the living room and sit next to Gray. Put her hand on his thigh. Or not.

She got up from her perch on the commode seat and went to look at herself in the mirror. Aside from the scars, she wasn't that bad. In fact, she had good eyes, and her hair worked. Then her gaze moved to her waist. *What if he really didn't care?* The thought made her shiver.

She pushed her hair from her temples. Checked her makeup. Grabbed a tissue to wipe a mascara smudge from beneath her eye. Her lipstick was in her purse, but then, if she did what she said she was going to do, lipstick wasn't necessary.

The woman in the mirror looked confident. And a little excited. Shelby smiled. Who was she kidding? Tonight, she was going to go for it. No backing off. No cold feet. She was going to make love to that exquisite male and build herself a memory that would last a lifetime. She was going to enjoy every second of it.

She unlocked the door and swung it open with all her determination. Then she stopped short, slammed the door shut and went to the sink. She picked up her purse, got out her makeup bag and found her travel toothbrush. One wanted clean, fresh breath when one was about to be ravished.

Finally, she really was ready to go out there. Well, almost. First, she needed a glass of water. Or maybe wine. She left the bathroom and hurried down the hall, moving faster and faster as she approached the kitchen. She heard the television from the living room, and she could picture him sitting on the couch, waiting for her. She pushed open the kitchen door and heard a sickening thud as the door stopped short.

"Umph."

She slipped inside to find Gray holding his nose. His moan didn't sound good. "Are you okay?"

He shook his head.

"Did I break it?"

He looked at the swinging door. "No," he said, his voice muffled by his hands.

"Not the door. Your nose."

He gently pressed his nose from top to bottom, grimacing, but only a little. "Nope."

"Ice," she said.

"Ice?"

"It might swell."

He shook his head. "I'll be fine." He took his hands down. "See? All better."

"Are you sure?"

He nodded. "Sure."

"I'm so sorry."

"Don't worry about it."

"I—"

He took her arms and pulled her toward him. "Don't worry about it," he repeated. "It was nothing."

She reached up and touched the bridge of his nose. He winced. "Nothing, my foot." Breaking free of his hold, she went to the freezer, and just as she was reaching for ice cubes, she saw the frozen bag of peas. She grabbed it and went back to Gray. "Use this."

"For what?"

"Tomorrow's breakfast. As a cold compress, silly."

"Oh. Right." He took the bag and brought it to his face. "It's cold."

"It's supposed to be."

"But I'm fine."

"Just do it. Five minutes."

"Shelby," he said as he shook his head. "You didn't hurt me. I promise."

"But—"

He stepped closer to her, making her bend her head back to see him. "I'll prove it to you."

His lips came down on hers. Gently at first, then the pressure increased. She was the one who moaned as his warm tongue probed her mouth, sending powerful signals to all the places in her body she wanted him to touch. Her nipples tightened, making her rub against his chest. She had to squeeze between her legs as the unique and unmistakable throb became stronger and stronger.

His hands moved down her back, but there was no time to worry about that as he shifted his position, angling his head more to the right. He moved her slowly backward. One step, then two. Until she came to the wall. Once he had her there, he pressed his advantage.

At first, she didn't know what he was doing, taking one hand in each of his own. But then she realized he was pulling them above her head. Holding them captive as his tongue worked its delicious mischief. He pressed himself against her, and she felt his hard length just under her tummy. Just above the source of her discomfort. A discomfort only he could ease.

He moved his mouth to her neck, and she let her head lean against the wall. She tried to move her hands, but he held her tight. The position wasn't scary. At least not in the way she would have guessed.

What frightened her was her own desire. The feral way her body moved as she tried to find release. Her breathing quickened as he lifted his head. But he didn't kiss her. She opened her eyes to find him staring at her. His gaze held her as firmly as his hands.

"Shelby, please..."

She understood. And yet something held her back. Some warning signal from deep inside.

"I want you," he whispered. "I want you in my bed."

She quivered, and the ache inside her doubled. And yet...

"I need to be inside you," he said, his voice low and gruff and his gaze burning with desire.

"I—"

"What?"

"I'm frightened," she said, amazed at her admission.

He let go of her hands. "Of me?"

She shook her head as she lowered her arms.

"Then what?"

"Of this."

His head tilted slightly. "I don't understand."

"This isn't something I, uh, usually do," she said.

"You don't think I know that?"

"You do?"

He nodded. "I've told myself a hundred times to leave you alone. I've failed miserably."

She swallowed the sudden lump in her throat. "Really? Even after—"

His smile was her answer. "I don't know what it is about you." He touched her hair, holding it between his fingers. "Maybe it's the color of your hair,'' he said, and then his gaze moved to meet hers. ''Or maybe it's those bedroom eyes.''

''I'm not—''

''Yes, you are. You're beautiful.''

She closed her eyes, hardly knowing what to do. The words—oh, how she'd longed to hear those words—and yet she didn't believe them. Not really.

He touched the bottom of her chin. ''Shelby.''

She looked at him.

''I'm telling you the truth.'' He grinned again. ''I don't know you well enough to lie to you.''

''Will you tell me one more thing, then?''

He nodded, his hand slipping behind her neck as if he meant to kiss her.

''Would you find me...beautiful...tomorrow? Or next week, when you're not stuck in the house with two four-year-olds?''

He sighed. ''Of course. Do you think I'm that shallow?''

''That's the problem. I don't know you at all. You could be shallow, you could be manipulative, you could be a terrible person.''

''If you truly believed that, you would have been out of here long ago. Even though I don't know you well, I do know one thing. You're an observer. And you're intuitive as hell. I bet everyone you know comes to you when they have a problem. Am I right?''

She shrugged a grudging yes.

''I thought so.''

''But that still doesn't mean I should...''

''Make love with me?''

She moistened her suddenly dry lips, then opened her mouth to speak, but nothing came out.

"Tell you what. Let's not worry about that right now. Let's just go put the kids to bed, then see what happens."

She knew exactly what was going to happen. She took his hand and led the way.

CHAPTER EIGHT

AFTER THE KIDS were tucked in, Gray followed Shelby into the living room. When they reached the couch, he sat down first, letting her decide how close she wanted to be. He marveled at his self-restraint. A few months ago he would have had her in his bed about ten seconds after the children were asleep. What had changed? This was the first time he'd been with a woman since he'd made the decision to straighten up. Could that be it?

He'd always been a man to take what he wanted. It had never particularly mattered what he had to do to accomplish his goal. As he looked at her, sitting about six inches to his left, the irony of the situation hit him. He was with a voluptuous, delectable female who was ripe for the picking, and he'd just developed a conscience. Good one.

She held the remote control in her small hand, pointing at the television as if it were a ray gun. She clicked and clicked until she saw Dennis Quaid. "Oh, yes. One of my favorite movies."

"What is it?"

The Big Easy.

"Never saw it."

She turned to him. "Are you kidding?"

He shook his head. "I rented the tape once. Forgot

about it. Ended up paying twenty-two dollars in late fines.''

"It's really good, only…''

"What?''

"There's this scene.''

"Yes?''

"Dennis seduces Ellen Barkin. It's, um, pretty erotic.''

He smiled at her. "You think I won't be able to control myself when I get a load of his moves, eh?''

She shook her head. "Not you. Me.''

"I like this movie already.''

She grinned, then sat back. His hand reached her neck, and for a few moments, while she caught him up on the plot, he rubbed her there. It was highly unsatisfactory. But if the mountain wouldn't move to Mohammed… "You want something to drink?''

She nodded. "That would be great.''

"Wine?''

She thought about it for a moment. "Sure.''

"Coming right up.''

"Hurry, though. You're going to miss everything.''

He got up, pausing to kiss her lightly as he rose. "I don't think I'm going to miss anything important.''

She blinked. "Oh.''

He hurried into the kitchen, but his haste had nothing to do with Dennis Quaid or Ellen Barkin. All he could think about was Shelby in his bed. The whole idea of sleeping with her was as intoxicating as anything he could think of. Maybe because they both knew they'd never see each other again. Or maybe it was because he suspected she not only wanted this, but needed it that made him want to give her the time of her life.

It reminded him of vacation sex. The kind where all inhibitions were thrown out the window because tomorrow you were booked on separate planes going who knew where.

He got the bottle of Merlot from his brother's wine rack, a couple of glasses and the corkscrew. Before he headed to the couch, he checked himself out on the shiny side of the toaster. After smoothing down a stray lock of hair, he nodded. He was primed and ready for action.

Shelby. What a kick in the ass she was. Bright, funny, intuitive, talented. She'd overcome so much. Everything except her own body image. Maybe, if he did it right, after tonight, she'd see herself as desirable. Because, damn it, she was.

He pushed open the kitchen door, stopping when he saw her. She hadn't moved, Well, not sideways. She had half risen from the couch. Her behind swayed a little to the right, then center, then a little to the left. He forced himself not to laugh. The poor kid couldn't decide where to sit. Closer? Farther? Now that wine was entering the mix, he felt sure the decision would be moot shortly. She sat down, put her face in her hands, then scooted an inch to her right.

Gray backed into the kitchen. He counted to ten, then he coughed, loudly, before he walked through the door once more. She'd leaned back, crossed her legs, thrown her arm casually over the back of the couch, looking for all the world as if she'd been bored silly waiting for him to get his act together. He smiled an apology as he put the wine accoutrements on the coffee table. "Sorry I was so long. Couldn't decide on the wine."

She looked at the bottle, telltale spots of pink on

each cheekbone betraying her nonchalance. "I like Merlot."

"Good. So what have I missed?"

Her eyes opened wide until she saw him nod at the television. She hemmed and hawed while he opened the wine, but by the time he handed her her glass, she'd figured out what was happening on the screen.

He hardly heard a word of her recap. He had no room for a movie, not when the drama on the couch was so compelling. Would she? Wouldn't she? He wasn't going to push, although from what he could see, all she needed was a stiff breeze to fall.

She sipped her drink, her gaze darting from him to the screen then back again. If she squeezed her glass much harder, he was afraid it would shatter. Something had to be done.

"So," he said, leaning back and slightly away from her. "What is it you like so much about this movie?"

Her immediate crimson blush told him it wasn't the plot.

"I don't know," she said. "The actors are really good…."

"The actors?"

She nodded, looked at the screen and nearly dropped her glass. He looked, and what he saw was highly intriguing. Ellen Barkin was on the bed with Dennis Quaid. They were both dressed. Dennis had his hand under Ellen's skirt, and it was obvious he knew what he was doing. Ellen was at the brink.

Gray got hard. Again. Painfully, achingly hard. His fingers itched to touch Shelby, to take Quaid's cue and turn the innocent miss to his left into a quivering mass of aroused female. His hand went to the back of the couch. He leaned to his left. The hotter the action got on the screen, the louder his libido got. The hell with being the nice guy. Nice guys finished last, right?

He touched Shelby's shoulder, and her whole body reacted as if he'd shocked her with an electric wire. The last thing Shelby needed was a nice guy. Oh, no. This woman needed a man who would rip away her inhibitions like wrapping paper. Who would appreciate the gift underneath. He moved closer.

SHELBY KNEW this was it. The moment of truth. She took a swig of wine for courage. Only, the wine went down the wrong way. She coughed as she put down the glass, coughed some more, then turned sharply away from him, gasping for control. Her pulse raced as she struggled, but finally, after what seemed like forever, the choking stopped. She took a deep breath, then shot off the couch.

"Shelby?"

"Yes?" she answered lightly, keeping her back to him.

"Are you all right?"

"Oh, sure. I'm fine. Just going to the rest room."

"Can I help?"

"No, I can go to the bathroom by myself."

"That's not what I meant."

She hurried on, not once looking at him. "Thanks, anyway!" Great. Just great. She could have been more humiliated, but she didn't see how. What a seductress! He was undoubtedly panting after her, anxious to see more of her patented Shelby style.

She closed the door to the bathroom and locked it. It took her a moment to gather her courage to look in the mirror. Finally, she did, and a raccoon stared at her. Big, dark circles of mascara, dripping, no less, made her look as if she'd gone two rounds with Tyson, and lost.

It was hopeless. She sagged on the counter, her spirits as low as they had been high the moment Gray had touched her shoulder. She'd been very clear what her next move was. Turn slowly to face him. Let her lips curl in an enigmatic smile. Look down shyly, but just for a moment, then let her gaze move up his chest, his neck, his face, until she found his eyes. She'd stay very still. After that was supposed to be the kiss that would lead the way to a night that would take them from strangers to lovers.

Yeah.

She turned on the water and washed her face, using a Teletubbie washcloth to wipe off her mascara. Of course she didn't have her makeup with her. So now she was the freckle queen with the red eyes, which had always drawn men to her like moths to a flame.

Why hadn't she left when she'd had the opportunity? She was a fool for thinking she was ready for a night like this. Well, like this was supposed to be. She sighed, wondering what she was supposed to do next. Walk out, smile brightly, talk about the weather? Turn the lights off?

Turn the lights off! Yes, yes. Oh, heavens, yes. She'd set the mood. Make him think she'd planned this all along. The only rub was that she intended to take this all the way, but she had no birth control. She wasn't on the pill and she'd left her unused diaphragm in some dusty corner of her bathroom. Would he be prepared? Sure. Men like him were. Weren't they?

She folded the washcloth in a small square and put

it on the sink. As she turned to leave, her eye caught on the medicine cabinet. It wasn't nice to snoop. She knew that. But maybe, just this once…

She pulled the cabinet door open an inch. That didn't help, so she opened it the rest of the way. And there it was. A box of condoms. It was a sign. An omen.

Shelby reached in, hoping against hope there was more than one packet. Not that she thought she'd need more, but she didn't want to leave his brother and sister-in-law empty-handed, so to speak. Tomorrow she'd replace it, regardless. It turned out that there were several packets, all of them orange, all of them with the unmistakable circular lump.

Another deep breath gave her the courage to leave the bathroom. She paused at the end of the hallway. He had his wineglass in his hand. His gaze was on the television screen. His demeanor casual. God, he was good-looking. He could be an actor if he wanted to. Or a model. No, he wouldn't be a model. Maybe a politician.

Okay. Enough chatter. She reached around the wall and groped until she found the light switch. It was a dimmer, and she turned it the wrong way, filling the room with light, bringing Gray's attention right to her. She scrambled to turn the light off, and when she succeeded, she considered getting her purse and driving to Dallas. But it was late, and she'd promised.

She walked toward him, making sure she didn't trip on any toys or her own feet. He smiled at her as she drew near. "You all better?"

She nodded. "Right as rain."

"Good. You were gone awhile."

"Emergency makeup repairs."

"Ah." He patted the seat beside him.

Shelby sat down right where his hand had been. So close, her arm pressed against his. She could see his face clearly, but she knew she was mostly in shadow. Excellent.

"Feel like trying it again with the wine?"

"No. Thanks."

He grinned. "Sure."

She smiled back, trying to look as relaxed as he did. But it wasn't easy. This situation was totally outside her experience. She felt more like an actress playing a part than Shelby Lord.

Her hand moved from her lap. Hovered for a few seconds while she told her inhibitions to take a hike. Then she actually did it. She put her hand on his thigh.

He jumped and nearly lost his grip on the wineglass. But she'd done it! She had her hand on his knee. Oh, well, actually a little higher than his knee. Definitely the upper third. Should she move it down? Leave it alone? Her heart pounded in her chest, worsening as her hand warmed with his heat.

"Shelby?"

"Yes?"

"Nothing."

She turned to him, doing her best to look like a seductress, like someone who slept with oodles of men then tossed them out like used tissues.

His smiled broadened. "Can I ask you a personal question?"

She nodded.

"Have you ever...?"

Her face heated in the billionth blush of the day. "Me?" She laughed as if the question was preposterous. Then she looked at him. "Well, um, not really."

"Not really?" he repeated, his voice higher than a moment ago.

"I mean, not technically." Her hand felt supersensitive. She could feel his muscles tense beneath her palm.

"Care to explain that one?"

"No."

"How old are you?"

"That's a pretty bold question."

"Look who's talking."

"I'm almost twenty-six."

"And you haven't…"

"No. I haven't."

"Oh."

She sighed. "As you can see, I'm not very good at this."

"No, no. You're fine. You're terrific."

"If I'm so terrific, why haven't you kissed me?"

He coughed. Put his glass on the coffee table. "I didn't know there was a time limit."

She pulled her hand back and used it to bury her face in. "I need to leave."

"What?"

She lifted her head a bit. But she didn't look at him. "I need to leave. I'm sure you'll find a sitter in the morning." With that pronouncement she rose, ready to run as far and as fast as her car would take her.

He caught her by the arm. "Shelby."

"What?"

"Don't go."

"I really need to go. So please, just let me."

He pulled her to him. Gently, but insistently, until she sat next to him once more. "I don't want you to go."

"Having fun, are you?"

"Yes. As a matter of fact, I am."

"Great. I've always wanted to be a court jester."

He touched her chin, turning her head until she was forced to look into his eyes. "I find you completely charming."

"Oh, please."

"I do. Charming and witty and lovely."

She pulled her head away from his touch. "Now I know you're lying."

He moved so quickly she only realized his intention as his lips touched hers. He kissed her. Tenderly. Sweetly. Then not so sweetly. The pressure grew as he leaned in. As he tricked her lips apart and slipped his tongue between them. Her eyes fluttered closed as one hand touched her back and the other went to her neck.

She touched her tongue to his, and the thrill inside her chest wiped away her hesitation. She kissed him, moving, tasting and touching in a dance they both somehow knew.

A few moments later Gray shifted her position, and she found herself leaning back until she was lying on the couch slightly sideways, and he was next to her, and they touched from chest to knee. His kisses deepened as her hands went around his neck and back, and then she felt his knee urging her legs apart. She obliged, and he used his leg to press against the hottest part of her. She gasped with the pleasure, and he began kissing her neck just below her ear. It was bliss. Better than her imagination could have conjured. He stroked her with strong hands, nearing but never quite touching, her sensitive breasts, driving her crazier by the moment. She ended up pressing her chest to him in an attempt to ease the ache.

He moaned, and his hot breath made her quiver.

He pulled back suddenly, a whispered curse startling her to her toes.

"What's wrong?"

"We need to stop this."

"What?"

"This."

She opened her eyes. "Why?"

"Because if we go on any longer, I won't be able to stop."

"Who asked you to?"

"No one. Me. Damn it, it's more complicated than I thought." He stilled his hands, and then he was gone. When she turned, he was already on his feet. "It's late. And I've run you ragged. Did you bring your suitcase in?"

His voice sounded so casual, so unaffected that a wave of shame washed over her. It was déjà vu. He'd probably pictured her naked. Her gaze moved down his body, and despite his dismissal of her, she could see quite clearly he wasn't turned off.

Shelby sat up. "What's going on?"

"Nothing."

"Then why…?"

He got his wine and polished it off. He'd turned so his back was to her. "I just don't think it's a good idea."

"It's because of my scars, right?"

"No." He turned to face her again, his grip on his

empty glass so fierce she thought he might break it. "God, no. I don't give a damn about that."

Although it was difficult, she almost believed him. "Is it because of being careful?" She reached into her pocket and pulled out one of the condoms. "I have this."

He sighed heavily and shook his head as if she was missing something terribly obvious.

"Well, then, what is it?"

"I can't. Okay? No, not that I *can't,* because of course I can, but I can't."

"What are you talking about?"

"Shelby, I can't. You're a—"

"Virgin?"

"Yeah."

"I'm not planning on joining a convent, Gray. And I am over twenty-one."

His hands went up in a gesture of pure frustration. "I know all that. I know how good it feels to kiss you, and how incredible it would be to do all the things I can't stop thinking about. But I also know it's just for one night, and that you're not a one-night kind of woman."

"I'm not?"

He shook his head, then sat next to her. "You know you're not."

"What if I tell you I want to be?"

"I'd tell you I don't believe you."

"Why is it so important to you? Unless it's just an excuse."

He let loose with a frustrated growl. "I don't understand it, either. Not that I'm proud of it or anything, but I've never put the brakes on like this before. Not ever. For some idiotic reason my conscience decided to come to life tonight. I'm as confused about it as you are.''

''Well. I guess that's that.''

''Yeah. Damn it, it is.''

She got her wineglass and took a few sips. Her gaze went to the television. She watched as a woman talked about feeling fresh. ''So it's all about you, right? Nothing to do with me.''

''Right. My problem. Not yours.''

She poured another half glass for herself and for him. Then she took a few sips. ''Any clue as to why this sudden fit of gallantry hit tonight?''

''Not a one.''

''Maybe the kids upstairs?''

''Maybe.''

''We did just meet yesterday.''

''Uh-uh. That's not traditionally a deterrent.''

''I, uh, couldn't help noticing it wasn't physical.''

He laughed. ''No. The plumbing is all in working order.''

''Hmm.''

''Yeah.''

She was watching a rerun of ''Sanford and Son.'' She hadn't even realized *The Big Easy* had ended. And if her memory served, it hadn't ended well for Dennis or Ellen, either.

''Shelby?''

''Yes?''

''I think I need to go to bed.''

''Oh?''

''My, uh, predicament isn't resolving itself the way I thought it would.''

It took her a long minute to figure out what he meant. Her gaze shot to his lap. He was right. Even from this angle she could see it was a *large* predicament. "Maybe I should just leave. I can make it to Dallas in a few hours."

"No. It's too late."

"I suppose." She looked at him, but his gaze was fixed on the TV. "Well, then. Guess I'll go on up."

He nodded, his gaze shifting from the TV set to her and back again.

"Night."

"Night."

"Gray?"

"Hmm?"

"For what it's worth, I think it would have been wonderful."

He moaned as he closed his eyes and shook his head. She made a discreet exit, only to remember halfway up the stairs that her overnight bag was still in the car.

CHAPTER NINE

GRAY TURNED ON the light. It was five in the morning, and he'd been up for an hour already. This, after getting to sleep well after midnight. Normally, he slept like a baby. But normally, he wasn't a colossal schmuck. Okay, so maybe he sometimes was a colossal schmuck, but at least it never used to bother him.

What the hell had he been thinking? She wanted it. She'd brought her own birth control. She'd practically thrown herself at him. But did he do what any normal, red-blooded American male would do? Oh, no. *He* had to be noble. *He* had to act like her friggin' mother.

His reward was a night of tossing and turning, his body letting him know that it didn't appreciate his Dudley Do-Right impression. His body understood that when a woman asked if he'd like to have sex, he should say *yes*.

He groaned as he climbed out of bed. His head hurt, his mouth felt like a cotton factory, and those were only his complaints above the waist. The shower beckoned so loudly that he put paste on his toothbrush and climbed under the hot water while he brushed.

As soon as possible he would call the baby-sitting agency. And if they couldn't help him, he'd call the National Guard. Shelby had to go.

He finished brushing his teeth and rinsed his mouth with hot water, then he got to work washing his hair. She had to go because he knew with utter certainty that if she offered again, he wasn't going to say no. In fact, he probably couldn't even wait for her to make the offer. He wanted her *now*.

He stopped washing his hair and quickly lathered his body. Then he turned to the spigots and gritted his teeth as he lowered the temperature. At first, it felt kind of good, but when he kept turning off the hot, the cold became icy, and all he wanted to do was get out of the damn shower. Instead, he forced himself to rinse off completely, to make sure his hair was squeaky clean.

A few moments later he turned off the cold, wondering if he'd done permanent damage. Thank God the big, fluffy bath sheet was right there or he'd have gone into hypothermia. He rubbed hard, prompting his circulation to kick into gear. After a long time, he felt human again, and ready to get on with his day.

His toiletries were on the counter, so he wrapped the towel around his waist and lathered up for his shave. Thoughts of Shelby kept trying to get into his head, but he ignored them. It was frustrating as hell, and this was only his imagination. What was it going to be like seeing her in the flesh?

He shaved his right cheek carefully, forcing himself to think about two things—the razor and the stubble. Period. No women allowed. Not even for one blasted second.

After he rinsed the razor and brought it up to his left cheek, something caught his eye behind him. He whirled around to find Jem and Scout standing like little soldiers at the bathroom door.

"There's no Rice Krispies," Jem said.

"And no Sugar Pops."

Gray checked his towel. "No cereal?"

The twins shook their heads in unison, as if they'd practiced before their entrance.

"Tell you what. Let me finish up in here, and then we'll find something to eat."

Scout frowned. "We want Shelby to fix us breakfast."

"Is she awake?"

Again, the two heads went from side to side as if they were connected.

"I think we can manage breakfast, okay?"

"I can make pancakes," Jem said. "I do it with Mommy all the time."

"Pancakes?" Gray felt a shudder of trepidation. "I was thinking more along the lines of toast with jam."

"Pancakes!" Jem shouted.

"Pancakes!" Scout echoed.

Gray frowned. Pancakes were a level-three breakfast. Level one was McDonald's. Level two was toast or cereal. Level three involved the stove. He didn't do level three.

"Why don't you guys go on downstairs and have some juice. I'll be down in a few minutes."

"I'll start the pancakes."

"You will do no such thing, Jem Jackson. Juice. Nothing but juice."

Jem kicked the door frame as he left, which Gray took as a good sign. But he shaved the rest of his face in a hurry.

By the time he was dressed and downstairs, the kids had managed to pretty much trash the living room. Lincoln Logs were all over the floor, and the dinosaurs had come out of the cupboard in force, threatening to devour the six or seven Barbies also strewn about. Jem had a juice box in one hand and a Nerf ball in the other. The way he was looking at Scout, Gray thought he might be aiming to throw one or the other at his sister.

"Hey, there, cowpoke. What ya up to?"

Jem jumped at his voice and dropped the ball. One disaster averted. And it was only ten to six.

"Shelby's still not awake?"

Scout looked up from the doll she was dressing. "No."

"So it's just us chickens, eh?"

"Huh?"

He grinned. "It's an expression, Scout. Not literal."

"What's literal?"

"Literal means real."

"But we're not chickens."

The way she looked at him, he knew that not only did she not understand, but she thought her uncle Gray was loco. "Let's go see about breakfast, huh?"

She forgot all about literal chickens and Barbie dolls and jumped up, running ahead of him through the swinging doors. Jem followed hot on her heels, and when Gray stepped inside, the two of them had the refrigerator door open.

"You still want pancakes, huh?"

"Yes!" they yelled, loud enough to wake the dead—and Shelby.

"Shh. Inside voices, please." He opened the pantry door, hoping Ellen had some prepared pancake mix on hand. It was a slim hope, but hey, she was the one who'd explained inside and outside voices to him.

Four-year-olds, as he could now testify, liked to yell. The louder, the better.

They also had about three times the energy of a normal human, which he could also testify to. They never seemed to stop. Ellen had tried to warn him, but he hadn't realized she meant they *never* stopped.

No pancake mix. No way he could make them from scratch. He came out to see three eggs dangerously close to the edge of the counter. He wasted no time plucking them from their perch. "Tell you what. I'm not sure I can do the whole pancake thing with you..."

Immediate groans and frowns filled the kitchen.

"...but I think, if we ask her nicely, Shelby can."

Jem kicked the fridge door. "She's asleep."

That was the problem, of course. But Gray had an inkling of an idea. A mean and rotten idea, but, hey, they wanted pancakes.

He shook his head at himself. This wasn't just about breakfast. Last night had ended like crap. God only knew what she'd think about him this morning. Coward that he was, he'd use the kids to break the ice.

"Come here," he said, leading the twins to the kitchen table. "This is what we're gonna do."

SHELBY PUSHED ASIDE the hanging tropical ferns and took another step on the leaves that carpeted the rich earth of the island. Her sarong caught on a low-lying branch, but she escaped unharmed. A few more steps with the breeze ruffling her long hair, caressing her flawless skin, and she came to the clearing.

He was there.

She smiled demurely, and Gray's eyes widened as

he looked at her slender body. He was dressed in a loincloth. Just a loincloth. She could see his entire chest with the sparse dark hair, his chiseled muscles flexing in the sun.

He waved her over, and she was surprised to see a brilliant pool of cool, blue water, fed by a waterfall that seemed as high as the sky itself. He touched her arms, and she lifted her chin. His smile told her he thought she was beautiful. Then, as he leaned down to kiss her, his hands found the two ends of her sarong, tied behind her neck, and in one swift movement, he'd loosened them so the whole garment fluttered to the ground.

Being naked in front of him wasn't embarrassing at all. In fact, she felt glorious. And thin. And normal. There were no scars, not a one. His hands on her warm flesh felt completely natural and sinfully sweet. He leaned down to kiss her, but the jungle drums stopped him. She tried to ignore the strange, disturbing jungle rhythm and concentrate on his kiss, but the drums got louder and louder, the noise deafening and a little scary. She turned to Gray, but he'd disappeared. She was naked, alone, and then the whole earth started shaking in a violent earthquake—

Shelby's eyes snapped open. The first thing she saw was Scout jumping up and down on her bed. The second thing was Jem banging on a pair of bongos with two rubber mallets. She jerked her gaze down, and to her relief she wasn't naked, but quite decent under the covers in her nightshirt.

"Good morning," she said, having to speak way more loudly than anyone who'd just been rudely awakened should have to.

"We want pancakes!" Scout shouted.

"Pancakes!"

Shelby covered her ears and grimaced, not even close to being prepared for this amount of noise. "Quiet!"

Jem hit the bongos twice, then stopped. Scout bounced on her butt, then off the bed. Just as she was going to ask the little darlings to leave, Shelby caught a glimpse of a tall, dark man outside the door. When she turned, the shape disappeared, but it was too late.

"Scout, Jem, did Uncle Gray tell you to come in here?"

Jem shook his head. Scout did, too, but then she said, "He told us not to tell."

"Oh, well, then you mustn't tell."

"Okay."

Shelby knew it. Gray was so busted. It must have been the pancakes. The wretched man probably didn't know how to make them and expected her to leap out of bed and cook for them all. Ha!

"Can you make pancakes?" Scout asked.

"Yes, I can. But we don't have everything we need to make them. But Uncle Gray will take us to breakfast, where you can order whatever you want."

"Yay!"

"Pancakes!"

She held up her hand to quiet the din. "But first, I need to get up and get dressed, so, Jem, why don't you go show Uncle Gray how wonderfully you play the bongos. Scout, you can get some lids from the pots and pans cupboard and play along with him."

"Okay," she said as she dashed out of the guest room. Jem followed right behind.

Once she was alone, Shelby closed her eyes, wondering if there was any possible way to get back to sleep, back to the island. But after a moment, she gave up trying. The unfortunate truth was that reality waited forever. She'd have to face Gray sometime today. At least she need only suffer the sting of his rejection through breakfast. And then she'd be gone.

GRAY SAW HER out of the corner of his eye, and he jerked his hand below the level of the table. But the look on her face told him it was too late. Besides, the evidence, about five pot lids and the damn bongos, was on the floor in front of her.

"Bribery?" she asked, her right brow arched disdainfully.

"Whatever works."

She sighed and shook her head as she moved toward the coffeepot. "Sure you made the coffee right? Or should I just dump it out and start from scratch?"

"Hey. I make great coffee." He handed the five-dollar bill to Scout, having already given Jem his. Although her words were meant to tease, Shelby sounded tense, uneasy. He shouldn't have pulled the stupid stunt with the kids. Or maybe she was still smarting from last night.

"Oh, so there are some things you can cook?"

He stood up and put his wallet in his pocket, then headed toward Shelby. "I make the best martini in the northern hemisphere."

"That's not cooking. That's mixing."

"I also make a particularly elegant sandwich that I made up all by myself."

She got a mug from the cupboard and turned to face him, leaning against the counter. "Oh?"

He nodded.

"Peanut butter and cheese."

She grimaced. "Do me a favor?"

"Hmm?"

"Never speak of that sandwich again."

He laughed, feeling much better. She'd relaxed, granting him absolution for his sins last night. But he'd better watch it or he might find himself alone with the little pancake-eating monsters.

She poured her coffee, sipped a couple of times, then sighed.

"See?"

"Yes. You do make good coffee."

He grinned, feeling stupid that her silly compliment felt so good.

"So did the kids explain to you about breakfast?"

He glanced behind him to find Jem at the kitchen table using the salt shaker as a race car. Jem provided the sound effects as he zoomed around the pepper mill and the napkin holder.

Scout was by the door, and for some bewildering reason she'd taken off her shirt and her shoes. "You mean did they tell me we're going out to breakfast?"

"Yep," Shelby said.

"Tell me something." Gray faced her again. "Why is Scout taking off her clothes?"

Shelby leaned sideways so she could see Scout. "Honey? How come you're taking off your clothes?"

"I don't like them."

"What do you want to wear?"

"Pokémon."

"Okay. Why don't you take your other clothes up to your room, put on your Pokémon and come back down. Hurry now, because we want to go get pancakes."

Scout gathered her belongings, all but one shoe,

and headed toward the stairs. Gray turned to Shelby.
"Humph."

"What?"

"It didn't occur to me to ask."

"Ah. Well, next time it will."

"Yeah."

She smiled, and a wave of desire nearly knocked him flat. This was nuts.

"I saw an International House of Pancakes on my way in," she said. "It was across the street from the grocery store. So what do you say we take care of breakfast and shopping in one trip?"

"Sure."

"Good. By the time we get back, you can call the agency again. See if you can get some help. I'll be leaving after lunch."

Disappointment displaced the desire in his gut. "Really?"

She nodded.

"I don't want you to go."

She hesitated. "It's the wise thing to do."

"Wise? *Wise?* Since when does that have anything to do with anything?"

Her laughter made things infinitely worse. Her hair shimmered as she turned to grab the coffeepot. He liked what she had on. It wasn't anything extravagant, just some black slacks and a T-shirt with the name of her diner, Austin Eats, emblazoned on the back. She looked comfortable in her sneakers, and she didn't glop on makeup or anything. She was just right.

"Scout will be down in a minute," she said. "We'll go in your car."

"I have a Z-3."

"Pardon?"

"It's a BMW—too small for all of us and definitely won't do the four of us and groceries."

"We'll take mine, then."

"So you can make a quick getaway after you drop us off?"

Her gaze lingered, and the easy smile faded.

He stepped closer. "What's wrong?"

She checked the kitchen table and Jem, then looked at him. "It's just, I **don't know**, different. Being here. With you."

"Different? How**?**"

"I'm not sure I can explain it. It feels like we've done this before. Hundreds of times. I keep thinking things about you that I have no business thinking."

It was his brow that rose this time.

"Not that kind of stuff. I mean, I was thinking of making cheeseburgers for lunch because you like them so much. And then it occurred to me that I have no idea if you like cheeseburgers."

"I do. I'm crazy about them."

"But I didn't know that."

"Maybe you're psychic."

She gave him a look. "Right."

"Okay, so maybe you just thought I was a cheeseburger type of guy."

"Even if that's true, it's kind of weird, don't you think?"

He opened his mouth to say something glib, then stopped. "Yeah. I do. I think this whole thing is kind of weird."

"For you, too, huh?"

"Last night—"

That wary, intense look shadowed her face. "Let's not go there."

"Okay. Only I just wanted to tell you that I'm not normally that way."

"What way?"

"Considerate."

She laughed. It sounded great.

"Don't worry. I won't notify the media. It'll be our little secret."

"Thanks. I have a certain reputation, you know."

"Hey, I don't usually proposition strange men. So I guess we're even."

"Am I?"

"What?"

"A strange man?"

"Oh, my, yes. But I meant it the other way. Strange as in unfamiliar."

He took in a deep breath, working hard to quell the intense urge to take her in his arms and kiss her senseless.

"We'd better go," she said, as if she'd read his mind. Who knows? Maybe she did. Maybe they'd known each other before, in a hundred other lifetimes. Not that he believed in that stuff. Maybe she was so easy to talk to because they were supposed to be together.

The thought shook him from his fugue state. What in hell was he thinking? Nuts. That's all. He was just plain nuts.

"SCOUT, HONEY, let me pour the syrup, please. Uh, wait!" Shelby sighed as she smiled at the beleaguered waitress. "Miss? I'm afraid we've had another mishap."

GRAY LOOKED at his ham and eggs. Or what used to be his ham and eggs. "Jem?"

"Yes?"

"It's not nice to loosen the top of the saltshaker. What ends up happening, you see, is that all the salt pours onto someone's plate."

"I'M SORRY," Scout mumbled just before she ducked to hide behind Shelby.

"Your turn, Jem."

"I'm sorry."

"Thank you." Shelby pressed a twenty into the waitress's palm. "I'm really terribly sorry. I don't know what got into them."

The waitress looked daggers back, then used both hands to wring out her wet hair. "Whatever."

GRAY LOOKED at the box of Twinkies, then at Scout. "Are you trying to tell me that your mother *wanted* you to get a box of Twinkies? Each?"

Scout nodded, but Gray wasn't sure. It didn't sound right at all.

"I'll take that." Shelby snatched the box from his hand and put it on the shelf. She turned to Scout. "Nice try." Then she pushed the cart to the end of the aisle.

"CLEANUP ON FOUR, please. Again."

CHAPTER TEN

GRAY BROUGHT IN the last of the groceries from the car and put the bags on the kitchen table. He slumped in the chair closest to him and looked at Shelby. She was smiling as she put away the groceries. Smiling! It wasn't possible. "How can you do that?" he asked.

"Someone has to. The milk would spoil."

"I don't mean that. I mean the smile. The energy."

"Come on, Gray, it wasn't that bad."

"Ha!"

"They're just doing what four-year-olds do. At that age, they have a terrific urge to see everything, touch everything. They're loud and insistent, and their imaginations are in full swing. It's quite remarkable, really."

"Remarkable."

She came over to the table and peered in the bags. Then she turned to him. "It'll be different when they're your children."

"How? Other than the fact that I'll be older and inherently less able to keep up with them."

"You'll find energy you didn't know you had. Trust me. As much as you love Scout and Jem, it can't compare to what you'll feel with your own."

"How would you know this?"

"I'm not sure. I think it has something to do with being a female."

He studied her for a long moment, and for about the fifth time that day he felt his insides tighten and his libido rev. "A very attractive female."

She shooed away the compliment, then pulled out two half-gallons of milk to take to the fridge.

"Why'd you do that? I meant it."

"I thought we weren't going there. You're the one that didn't want any hanky and, if I'm not mistaken, no panky, either."

Her teasing had taken on a light note, which made him feel freer to tease back. "Not even a little panky?"

"Nope. Well, not until the food's put away, at least."

He bounded out of his chair with renewed strength and determination. In his haste to get the groceries stowed, he nearly dropped the carton of eggs, but it was worth it to hear her laugh. In all his years of dating, he'd never been with anyone who laughed like Shelby. Not just the sound, but the abandon. If she were his, he'd make her laugh all the time.

"Gray, I'll finish up in here. Why don't you go make sure Jem and Scout are playing nicely. It's too quiet in there."

He closed the fridge door. "All right. But remember what you said."

"I was joking."

He moved over to where she stood, grabbed her around the waist, pulled her close and kissed her hard. Damn, but she tasted good. Smelled good. Felt good. The last thing he wanted to do was let her go, but he did. "I wasn't," he whispered just before he headed for the living room.

SHELBY WATCHED him leave, then stared at the swinging doors until they'd stopped swaying. When she was sure he wasn't coming back, she sagged against the table. What a morning! Jem and Scout had provided some much-needed distraction, but her awareness and her reaction to Gray were more than she could stand.

Everything he did made her want to rip off her clothes and yell, "Take me! Take me now!" She had the feeling it wouldn't have gone over well at the grocery store, and it might not have had the desired effect on Gray, either. But my God!

His hands. She'd been mesmerized as he'd cut up Scout's pancakes. His long, thick fingers sent her mind right to the gutter. No rings. Great watch. Just the right amount of hair. Tanned skin. Good grief, she must be going crazy.

Yes. That was it, of course. He was driving her crazy. His smile. The way he laughed. When he'd winked at her, she'd almost embarrassed herself in front of the waitress.

Oddly, it wasn't just his looks that had her walking around like a rabbit in heat. She loved his sense of humor. They talked as if they'd talked forever. She'd told him all about the remarkable events that had occurred in the last year. She'd shared the painful details of her years of recovery. He hadn't even blinked. But why would he? She was going to leave in a little while—as soon as she put away the food and cooked up a few entrees for the fridge.

God, she was stalling. He probably knew it, too. How pathetic she must look to him. She didn't need to make anything. He wasn't that helpless. But she wanted to stay. She needed to go. The longer she was near him, the worse the problem became. It was going to be difficult to return to her old life, and it was only a couple of days since they'd met.

Not good. Not wise. She was letting her imagination get the better of her, and all that could lead to was disappointment. She'd had enough of that, thank you. It was a shame, though, that he didn't live closer to Austin. Not that she thought they would get together if he did, but they could be friends. This giddy adolescent crush would fade, given time. Then there would just be the wonderful conversations, the laughter.

She put the rest of the food in the fridge, her movements careful so she didn't drop anything. Her thoughts were all about Gray. About a future that couldn't be.

The phone rang. Shelby wasn't sure if she should answer it or not, but Gray came through the swinging doors on the third ring.

He grabbed the receiver. "Hello."

His smile made her think it was his brother on the phone.

"Fine. Great."

He listened for a minute, rolled his eyes at her as he said, "They haven't been any trouble. Honest. They've been, uh, energetic, but at this age they have a terrific urge to see everything, touch everything. They're loud and insistent and their imaginations are in full swing. It's quite remarkable, really."

She shook her head at him, but then his smile was gone and his attention was fully on his conversation.

"What does that mean?"

Oh, no. It must be about his sister-in-law. The tests…

"Just do what you need to do. I'm fine here, and so are the kids. I swear, if anything happens I'll call. But I have terrific help."

She busied herself washing the counters, realizing how rude she'd been to eavesdrop. Of course, she could leave the room…. Nah.

"Right. From the agency. I'll tell you all about her when you get back. Don't worry. A week is nothing. It's all under control. Now, tell me about this test."

Shelby slipped out of the kitchen. She didn't want to intrude on something that personal. Interesting that Gray had said she was from the agency. Actually, it was smart. It sounded as if his brother and sister-in-law had enough to worry about. For Gray to agree to watch the twins for a week said a lot about the situation, and even more about the man. Despite his fears, his upcoming interview, he hadn't hesitated one second.

Jem and Scout were busy playing with the stuffed animals that blanketed the living room, and although they could both do with a good wash, they were happy. No need to rock the boat. Shelby went into the guest room and got her cell phone. She dialed the restaurant, and her new chef, Joe, answered on the second ring.

"Shelby! What's cooking?"

She grinned at Joe's worn-out pun. "Nothing. Which, I hope is not the case where you are."

He laughed in that deep way of his. "Nope. We've got a nice lunch crowd today. It's meat loaf Wednesday, remember?"

"Right."

"So, what's up? Just calling to see if the place was still running?"

Shelby exhaled slowly. "Actually, I was calling to hear how much you all miss and need me."

Joe laughed. "Should've saved your money. Everything's under control. Mary Jane came by yesterday. She's checking up on me and the crew. If we need anything, I can call her."

Shelby sat on the edge of the bed. That wasn't the response she'd expected. "Are you sure?"

"Quit worrying. The only thing you're in charge of is having a good vacation. We've got you covered."

"Thanks, Joe. I appreciate it."

"No sweat."

Shelby said goodbye, then hung up the phone, knowing she'd wanted someone else to make her decision for her. Gray needed her. But she needed to get as far away as possible. There was no getting around the fact that he was dangerous. The thought of him was enough to make her swoon. *Swoon.* It sounded like such an antiquated word, but it was accurate. She felt light-headed, dizzy, completely unglued when he so much as walked by her. That was the problem. Gray's need for her had to do with the kids. Her need for him was something else altogether.

She put her phone on the dresser and looked at her suitcase. How could she even think about staying? She simply didn't have enough clothes.

A loud thump from downstairs got her moving, and fast. But halfway down she saw the living room chair on its back, and she relaxed. No one was hurt. However, all was not peaceful among the dinosaurs. Scout had a Barbie body in one hand, a Barbie head in the other. Naturally, the little girl was upset. Jem seemed innocent enough on the floor with his blue Tyrannosaurus Rex, but Shelby thought his smile was a little too smug.

"Jem," she said as she reached the living room. "Could you come here, please?"

He didn't stand, choosing instead to stay on his hands and knees. But he did come.

"Jem, did you hurt Scout's Barbie?" She kept her voice low, just between the two of them.

"No."

"Are you sure?"

He growled like a dinosaur, attacked her leg with the small head of the toy, then frowned. "I didn't do it on purpose."

"What happened?"

He shrugged.

"I see. Well, let's try real hard not to hurt any toys again. Okay?"

He nodded, turned and crawled back to his dinosaur corral.

Shelby went to Scout and led her to the couch. They sat next to each other as Shelby reattached Barbie's head. Scout sniffed the whole time. Finally, Shelby handed the doll back. "All better."

"She is not."

"Why not?"

"He broke her."

"Yes, he did. But you know what?"

"What?"

"Sometimes these things happen. Jem didn't mean to hurt your doll, or you. He was just being a little boy."

"Little boys are poopy."

Shelby held back a grin. "Sometimes. But sometimes little girls are poopy, too."

"Nah."

"Now, Scout. I was a little girl once, too. So I know."

Scout frowned. "I wish he'd go away."

"You'd miss him something awful if he did."

"No, I wouldn't."

It was no use arguing. "I'll bet you're getting pretty tired, huh?"

Scout leaped off the couch. "No, I'm not. I'm not tired." She raced to the far corner of the living room, where she dropped to her knees in front of Barbie's Dream House.

Shelby figured she'd give them another half hour or so, then they'd need to eat lunch and take a nap. Which didn't sound like a bad idea for her, either. Except she had a decision to make.

WHAT HAD HE gotten himself into? Gray studied the contents of the newly filled fridge, but he didn't really see anything. His mind was too busy reeling over the prospect of taking care of the kids for a week. By himself.

What a moron. He should have told Ellen the real situation. Maybe she had a friend who could have come to help. No. She had enough to worry about with all those blood tests.

He thought about getting a beer, then changed his mind. He closed the door and went to his seat at the table. If only Shelby could stay. She was so damn good with the kids. She knew how to cook and she knew how to stop the arguing. She was also damn good company, and except for that one little thing, she was perfect.

Only the one little thing wasn't so little. No way

in hell he'd be able to keep his hands off her if she stayed. Not even for one night. It was like he'd been possessed or something. His attraction to her was all out of proportion. Knowing that didn't help. He just kept on wanting her.

The truth was, he needed her expertise. Her woman's touch. Her skill.

He needed her body in his bed.

Oh, hell.

As if his personal torment wasn't enough, Shelby chose that moment to walk into the kitchen. He smiled. He hoped it looked real.

She glanced at the empty bags from the grocery store. The coffeepot with this morning's cold coffee still in it. The floor where Scout had spilled some cereal. "Well?" she asked.

"Well, what?"

"Why are you sitting there? The trash needs to go out. There's at least two batches of clothes that need washing, and then there's lunch to prepare."

"Oh."

"So?"

"I can do that trash thing."

She laughed. "I wasn't offering you a choice. It all needs to get done."

"But—"

"And I have to leave. It's getting late."

He opened his mouth, prepared to beg her to stay. But then he closed it again. The desire for her was inescapable, and he had no business messing with her life. She should leave. She should have left yesterday. "Okay. I'll get right on it."

She glanced at the utility room. "When's the last time you did laundry?"

"I do laundry all the time."

Her gaze went to him, challenging the veracity of his statement.

"Okay, so I let my dry cleaner do my laundry. It's not calculus. I can figure it out."

"Of course you can. You're a very intelligent man."

"Thank you."

"And I'm sure you can figure out how to cook, too. It's only a week."

He felt his throat constrict as the panic bubbled up inside him. "No sweat."

"Gray?"

"Yeah?"

"It's all right. You'd better breathe again before you pass out."

"Does that mean you're staying?"

The urge to give in, to tell him she'd take care of everything, was strong. But had she learned nothing? Patterns. They could only be broken if she was willing to change. She'd be doing them both a favor by leaving. She gave him a sad smile and shook her head.

The earnest disappointment in his eyes almost made her renege. She quickly looked away and picked up a sponge to wipe the counter. "I hope your sister-in-law is all right."

"We're not sure. They have to get a biopsy."

"Oh, no."

He nodded.

"I really respect the fact that you're willing to take on the responsibility of the twins."

"But not enough to stay?"

She finished wiping the counter and tucked the

sponge behind the faucet. "One has nothing to do with the other."

"This is about last night, isn't it?"

"Not at all."

He sighed with relief. "Good."

"The thing is, I still want to… Oh, damn it. You're driving me crazy."

"I am?"

"You know you are."

He walked toward her, and she backed up.

"All the more reason I should leave," she said.

He stopped a foot away. "You think I can't control myself?"

She wanted to laugh. As if it was him she had to worry about. "I think you may be trying to seduce me into staying so I'll take care of the kids."

"Ouch." He put a hand to his heart. "That hurts."

She really had wounded him. The proof was in his eyes.

"Want to know what I think?" she asked, her head tilted so she could look him straight in the eye.

"Uh-huh."

"You're going to be just fine. You'll have the kids wrapped around your finger in no time."

He snorted. "You're dreaming. Besides—"

"You know I'm right. You don't need me."

"You're wrong."

She smiled sadly. "I'll get my bag. It's already packed."

"Shelby." He grabbed her arm and drew her to him. "I want you to stay. And it's not about the kids. Well, not just about the kids." One side of his mouth lifted, and his gaze touched her lips. "Is there anything I can do or say to get you to stay?"

The door behind him swung open, and Scout marched in. "Jem puked."

CHAPTER ELEVEN

GRAY SETTLED onto the couch, more tired than he'd been in a long time. Jem's fever had finally broken, and he was able to keep down some juice. Scout had spent an hour complaining of an upset stomach, but Shelby determined it was more of a cry for attention that anything else. Especially since the little angel had wolfed down two cups of popcorn while watching *Aladdin* for the hundredth time. The kids had finally fallen asleep by ten. He hoped that meant they wouldn't be getting up at the crack of dawn.

Bless Shelby for staying one more night. Even though she assured him Jem's fever was mild, Gray didn't know how he could have handled everything without her.

He glanced at her. She sat hugging the opposite end of the couch. "Did I remember to thank you for all this?"

"Wait till you get my bill," Shelby said, her tired gaze on the television. She sat with her legs curled under her, her bare feet peeking from beneath her butt. They were cute feet, and his gaze kept sliding to them. He'd never been particularly interested in feet before, so why he couldn't stop looking was a mystery.

"Name your price."

The corner of her mouth twitched. It was a mischievous twitch that stirred his curiosity.

"What?"

"Nothing."

"Nothing, my eye. What's spinning around in that pretty head of yours? You have some kind of repayment in mind, don't you?"

She glanced at him, then away. "I was teasing."

"Right."

She turned back with a glare. "Why? What do you think I meant?"

He tried to keep a straight face. "I'm not sure. Explain."

"There's nothing to explain," Shelby said. "I stayed to help with Jem because I wanted to. I didn't expect anything in return."

He reached for her hand. "Hey, I was just teasing, too."

"I know." She sighed. "Guess I'm tired. I'd better get to bed. I'm getting an early start tomorrow."

His grip tightened. "How early?"

She glanced at his hand, squeezing hers. "When I get up."

He tugged until she was forced to move close. "When?"

"After breakfast, and not a moment later."

He drew her closer still, ignoring her sharp intake of breath. "I'm sorry. I didn't hear you. When are you leaving?"

She cleared her throat. "After lunch."

He looked into her green, innocent eyes. The blush on her cheeks made her hair seem redder, her mouth more lush. "I think I have to kiss you."

"Oh."

"But—"

Her eyes widened in anticipation. Her pulse hammered beneath his thumb.

"The thing is… I want to make love with you, Shelby. More than you could ever imagine."

She bit her lower lip. He doubted she was aware of it. And she certainly couldn't have known what the small act had done to him. His body came to attention, just as it had all day, every time he looked at her or thought about her. No longer able to stand it, he scooted over until their bodies touched. He took her hand in his.

"There's this voice inside my head," he told her. "A pretty damn loud voice."

"What's it saying?"

"I think you already know."

She nodded slowly. "But what if it's wrong?"

"Is it? Really?"

Her gaze met his, and for a long time she just looked at him. Then she closed her eyes, and her long lashes brushed the very tops of her cheeks. "It might be right," she whispered. "It might be an awful mistake. I just don't know."

"There's the rub," he said, stroking her palm with his hand. "I don't know, either."

"So we probably shouldn't do anything." She visibly swallowed. "Right?"

He shook his head. "You got me. This is all new territory. I'm usually the one convincing the girl to hop into my bed, not stay out of it."

"Why is it so different this time?"

He brought her hand up to his mouth and gave her a gentle kiss. "I have no idea."

"Maybe you don't really want me."

He laughed. "Honey, there are wrong answers and then there are *wrong* answers."

Her smile blossomed, although he could still see a hint of disappointment. "All right. I believe you."

"Good."

She slipped her hand from his. "Guess I'll turn in, then."

"No, don't."

"Hmm?"

"It's too early. Don't go."

She got up, uncurling her lovely legs, then bent and kissed him on the cheek. Her scent wafted over him, making him dizzy with desire. His hand moved to stop her again, to stop this nonsense about waiting. But she stepped away. "I'll see you in the morning, Gray."

He cursed himself for a fool as she headed toward the stairs. An idiot who didn't deserve to be called a man. But then his senses returned as she stepped out of view. He honestly wasn't sure what the hell was going on, but for tonight, he'd keep his word. He wouldn't go to her room. He wouldn't take her in his arms. He wouldn't make love to her until the sun came up.

Of course, he'd probably need hospitalization by tomorrow morning. Even worse, by tomorrow afternoon she'd be gone.

SHOULD HE KNOCK? Two in the morning. *She's asleep. Of course, she's asleep.* Gray brought his arm down, yet he didn't leave. He stared at the door to the guest room. Maybe if he looked long enough he would be able to see inside.

He'd slept, but only for a few hours. Then Shelby

had awakened him, not in body but in spirit. However, the body had been along for the ride, and he'd imagined every inch of her in torturous detail.

What was the matter with him? It was insane. Utter madness. She wanted him, he wanted her. They weren't teenagers, for God's sake. They were consenting adults. Only, he couldn't consent. Some wire in his brain had come loose, and there didn't seem to be a way to fix it.

Maybe he should go back to bed. But maybe she was lying awake, thinking sexy thoughts. Maybe she was just as frustrated as he was.

He lifted his arm once more, determined to get on with it. But he didn't knock. Lord, how he wanted to, but he didn't.

SHOULD SHE GO to his room? It was late, only a little after two. Surely, he was sleeping. Besides, he had made himself perfectly clear. He wasn't interested. No, that wasn't right. He was interested, just not willing. So…what? Was she going to attack him? Jump on him as he slept?

But wasn't it just possible that he'd changed his mind? That if she showed up in her nightshirt, he'd…

She shook her head, amazed at herself. Shocked at her own thoughts, her inability to accept the situation for what it was.

He didn't want to sleep with her. Period. The end. It was time to get back in bed and go to sleep. Forget him. Forget the desire that was burning a hole inside her. Just stop thinking of him as anything more than a friend.

She turned from the door and walked to the still unfamiliar bed. It was her own fault. She never should have stayed. She should have gone when she'd had the chance. He could have handled Jem. Had she wanted the excuse to stay? It was too late to worry about that now. The only thing she could do was stop wanting him.

Yeah, right.

THE NEXT AFTERNOON, after lunch had been eaten and the dishes done, and the kids had gone down for their nap, Shelby had her purse in one hand and her car keys in the other. Her suitcase had already been stowed in the trunk. She was leaving. For real. Gray couldn't remember feeling more down.

He wanted to kiss her. Beg her to stay. Getting down on his knees had worked once before....

"Well, then, I guess I have everything." She glanced around the living room. Everywhere but at him.

"If you've forgotten anything I could always send it to you."

She smiled. It wasn't a very enthusiastic effort.

"Hell, maybe I could even take it to you myself," he said, and her smile wavered.

"That's sweet, but unnecessary. I haven't left anything."

He folded his arms across his chest.

"But here." She pulled out a piece of scrap paper and jotted down her cell phone number. "If anything happens to the kids, you can call me."

He took the paper, an idea already forming—

"A real emergency, Gray."

He deflated like a balloon. "Will you call me when you get to Dallas? So I know you got there okay?"

"Of course."

"I mean, you'll want to know how Jem's doing, too."

She pushed back her hair, her hand shaking slightly. "I said I'd call."

"Right." He followed her to the door. "Shelby?"

She stopped but kept her back to him. "Don't, Gray."

For once in his life he was at a loss for words. When she finally glanced at him, he nodded. Gave her a reassuring smile. Kept his hands to himself.

She walked to her car. He watched every step, wanting to call her back. Wanting…

The car door slammed. The engine revved. Her car, a nice black Maxima, moved down the drive and onto the street. He watched until she disappeared.

It wasn't over, he reminded himself. He had several hours before she called. Several hours to come up with a reason she had to come back. Something she wouldn't dismiss out of hand.

But what was he going to do as he plotted? He should take a nap. God knows he hadn't slept last night. He was achingly tired, yet he wouldn't feel comfortable sleeping now. What if the twins woke up? He headed for the kitchen. Another cup of coffee.

As he poured the hot java into his mug, his gaze fell on the telephone. Before he even thought things out, he'd picked up the receiver and dialed Kate's number.

It rang two times, then his sister answered. "Hello."

"Kate."

"Gray! How are you? Are you still at Ben's? How's Ellen doing? Is she all right?"

"I'm fine. Yes, yes and yes."

"Ha, ha. Come on, talk to me."

"I'm trying. But you won't shut up."

"I've missed you, too."

Gray took the phone and his mug to the table and settled in. Kate would know what he should do. She was a wise woman, his sister.

It didn't take long for him to fill her in. First, with what was going on with Ellen, then the kids, then the job, and finally, the situation with Shelby.

When he finished, he took a swig of coffee. It was lukewarm and bitter. How long had he been talking?

"Well, I'll be a monkey's uncle," Kate said.

"What?"

"I didn't think it was possible, but there you go. Living proof that people can change."

"Kate, what are you talking about?"

"You. You've finally gotten past puberty. I really should call the media. This is major."

He shook his head as he carried his cup to the microwave. "I didn't call you to be made fun of," he said as he pressed the buttons to set the machine for forty seconds.

"I know. But the opportunity presented itself, and I couldn't let it pass."

"Kate, do me a favor."

"What?"

"Shut up and tell me what's going on."

She laughed. "I've missed you!"

"Yeah, yeah. Come on. Spill."

He heard her sigh, and he wondered what she'd been doing when he'd called. He hadn't asked her anything about her life.

"Here's what I think," she said. "Seriously. I

think that your years as a wastrel are over. You've leaped into a major new cycle. You're trying real hard not to be the irresponsible kid you've been your whole life. You're growing up.''

''I'm the same age as you, sweetheart.''

''I know. But I matured faster than you. Even faster than Ben, but he caught up after the kids were born. It's about time you joined us in the world of adulthood.''

''Okay, even if I buy this cockamamie theory of yours, that doesn't explain why I let her walk out of here.''

''Duh, of course it does. Sheesh.''

The microwave dinged, and Gray got his coffee. ''How?''

''Come on, bro. You know this already. Grownups take responsibility for their actions. They know that sleeping with someone is significant. It shouldn't be done lightly. Grown-ups don't have to satisfy every urge the second it rears. And exceptional grown-ups think more about their friends than they do about themselves.''

He stared at the steam rising from his cup. ''Exceptional, huh?''

''Don't get all cocky about it. But yeah. This is a good thing, Gray. It may not feel so hot, but it is. Mom would be proud.''

He closed his eyes for a long moment. ''Okay, now tell me how to get her back.''

''As in permanently?''

''Don't get crazy on me.''

She snorted. ''Well, I guess that depends on how badly you want her.''

"I'm listening."

"You could tell her you're ready for a committed relationship."

"Or I could just be committed."

"Come on. Are you serious about this or what?"

"I don't know. I've got this job coming up. My five-year plan. She's got her life in Austin. I don't see how it could work."

"If you want it to work, it will."

He knew Kate believed that. But all he could see was one roadblock after another. "Thanks, kiddo."

"It's what I'm here for."

"So when are you coming to visit?"

"Soon."

"What does that mean?"

"I'm not sure. I have this whole work thing going on."

"And?"

"And that's all. I promise, I'll get there as soon as I can."

"Okay," he said. "I miss you."

"Ditto. Kiss the kids for me. And trust yourself, okay? You're on the right track. Just keep your eyes on the road and not the rearview mirror."

He said goodbye, then hung up the phone. For a long while, he sat at the kitchen table. He didn't touch his coffee. He thought about his mother, about the last few years. About Shelby, and Lattimer.

He hoped Kate was right. That his mother would be proud of him. At least for this. As for the rest? He had a long way to go. Instead of obsessing about Shelby, he needed to focus on Lattimer and getting the job.

SHELBY SHIFTED her shopping bags to her left hand as she headed to her car. She idly glanced at the stores she passed, and her gaze locked onto a stunning baby carriage. Immediately she came to a halt. It was blue and white, roomy, yet not too big. The canopy had perfect blue and white fringe all around, and there was space for a diaper bag and toys and—

A woman's image reflected next to her in the window stopped her. Her reflection showed a swollen belly, ripe with a child. Shelby's hand went to her stomach, and she just plain ached for a baby of her own. It had been so wonderful being with the twins. At home, all her friends had children or were planning children, and she'd been out here playing house with a man she'd never see again.

Her spirits sagged heavier than the black, rain-filled clouds darkening the sky. It was ironic that she'd chosen to come to the mall even though it was out of the way. She needed a few things now that she'd decided to go to Dallas. More important, she needed time to compose herself before her long drive.

She'd known it was going to be hard leaving Gray. She hadn't been prepared for how hard.

And because she clearly enjoyed torturing herself at every opportunity, she walked into the baby store. Everything she looked at might as well have had a sign that said Not For Shelby.

A wild thought came to her. What if she went back for one more night? And what if… It was strictly hypothetical of course, but what if she seduced Gray but didn't use one of those condoms she'd found in the medicine chest?

It was a nutty idea for sure, but still. He wouldn't have to know. Hell, she probably wouldn't get pregnant, anyway. The odds were astronomical. And yet, there was a chance. What if she got pregnant? She'd be a single mother. Was that so terrible? She had so many dear friends who would help out. Her brothers and sister would always be there for her to turn to. Financially, it was viable. She had that spare room she could easily turn into a nursery.

She wandered up and down the aisles, touching a blanket here, a crib there. Sighing over bibs and bottles, little tiny bathtubs. With every step, the idea inside her blossomed from a tiny seed to a garden of possibilities. She could do this. She could. But should she?

"May I help you?"

Shelby whirled at the sound of the woman's voice. It was the salesclerk. Shelby had seen her a few moments ago. She seemed nice, not at all pushy. With her salt-and-pepper hair and her wire-rimmed glasses she seemed a perfect grandma. She even smelled faintly of talcum powder. "I was just looking. Thank you."

"I won't bother you then. But if there's anything you need, please let me know."

Shelby smiled, and the woman smiled back. Just as she turned to help another customer, Shelby touched her arm.

"Yes?"

"I was wondering if you know of a baby-sitting service in the area."

The woman's brow creased as she thought. "There's Child Minders."

"Nope, we've tried them."

"I don't know of another service. But I sit from time to time. I only work here once a week. I'm usually free most evenings.''

"Seriously?''

The woman nodded. "I've got plenty of references from families around town. I can get you a list, if you like.''

"Do you have it here?''

"I think I do. Let me go check my bag.''

The woman—Shelby hadn't even gotten her name—was gone just a few moments. Enough time to make Shelby doubt her own sanity. Just seconds ago she was planning to seduce Gray into giving her a child. Now she was taking away the last possible reason for him to need her. What was it going to be?

"Here you are,'' the woman said, handing Shelby a neatly folded piece of paper. On the top was the woman's name, Sarah DeWitt. The list of her clients filled three columns on the eight-and-a-half by eleven-inch page.

"I'm Shelby Lord. But I won't be calling you. A man named Gray Jackson will.''

"Jackson? Is he any relation to Ben and Ellen Jackson?''

"Yes. He and Ben are brothers.''

"I've stayed with the twins once or twice. They're charming children.''

Shelby smiled and thanked her, looked around the baby store one more time, then walked out. That was it, then. Gray didn't need her. Not with Ms. DeWitt so handy. She could leave with a clear conscience. Be in Dallas before midnight.

She got to her car, tucked the paper in her purse, loaded the back seat with her packages, then slumped against the door. She looked at the darkening sky. It was going to rain. She was still only about six miles from the house. Maybe she shouldn't head for Dallas yet. Maybe she should stick around until the weather cleared, get a fresh start in the morning.

Maybe she should quit looking for an excuse to go back to Gray.

Shelby straightened and stuck the key in the ignition. There was no going back. She knew that. She just didn't like it.

CHAPTER TWELVE

"WHERE'S SHELBY? I want her to make us dinner."
Jem marched into the kitchen with Scout right behind
him. He was back to his old self, throwing things,
tormenting his sister and giving Gray a headache.

"She's never coming back." Scout flopped on a
chair, folded her small arms across her chest and
stuck out her lower lip. "Uncle Gray made her go
away."

Gray sighed. "How about cheeseburgers for dinner?" As soon as the words left his mouth, he was
hit with another wave of depression.

Shelby had known how he liked his cheeseburgers.
He hadn't told her. She'd just known. She was intuitive about a lot of other things, too. About the kids.
She'd only been gone for three hours, and he already
missed her like crazy.

"Why did you make her go away?" Jem looked
at him with large, wounded eyes. "We liked Shelby."

"I didn't make her go away. She had to leave. She
had to go to Dallas." Gray tried to smile, but the truth
was, he probably had chased her away.

From the moment he'd met her, she'd done nothing
but give. He'd been more than happy to take. Just
like always. As if it was his due.

Gray crouched to Jem's level. "Shelby is on vacation. She has other things to do besides hang around

here. But she'll call us later, and I'll let you talk to her, okay?''

Jem nodded, and Scout reminded Gray that she wanted to talk to Shelby, too.

He stood, his gaze straying to the phone. Only it wasn't there. ''Jem?''

''Huh?''

''Where's the phone?''

''Oops.''

Gray didn't like the sound of that *oops*. He also didn't like the way Jem scrambled from his chair and hightailed it out of the kitchen.

''Jem did it,'' Scout said, adding to Gray's sinking feeling.

The boy came back a moment later. In each hand, he held a piece of the phone. The casing and the innards. ''It broke.''

''How did it break?''

Jem shrugged.

Gray sighed as he put the unit together. It snapped into place, and when he pressed the button, he heard a dial tone. What if Shelby had tried to call him?

Maybe he ought to call her, just in case. Make sure she'd found the freeway in the rain. The storm was really picking up juice. Did her car have enough gas?

No. He wouldn't call her. He'd wait for her to call him. And when she did, he wouldn't say a word about her coming back. He wouldn't lie or even stretch the truth. She was gone, and that was that.

''Are we still having cheeseburgers?'' Jem asked.

''Sure. You want to help?''

Jem's eyes grew large again. ''Okay.''

Gray grinned as he went to the fridge. Funny, he wasn't so scared of them anymore. They weren't the terrible mystery he'd imagined. Shelby had taught him that. She'd taught him a lot of things.

The phone rang as he got out the cheese and mustard. Scout dove for it at the same time he did. He won. "Hello?"

"Hi."

"Shelby?"

"Uh, you busy?"

"I'm about to make cheeseburgers." His pulse sped up like a schoolgirl at her first dance. "Are you in Dallas already?"

"Not exactly."

"Good. It's too wet out there to drive fast."

She laughed softly. At least he thought she did. It was a bad connection.

"You made it out of here just in time. It's been pouring rain since you left."

He settled on a kitchen chair and waved the wildly gesticulating twins away. They'd get their turn with Shelby after he was finished.

"You said!" Jem grabbed for the phone.

"Me, too!" Scout pushed her brother out of the way.

Gray stood to keep the phone well out of reach. "Knock it off, you two." He put his mouth to the phone and wandered toward the window. "Sorry. The kids want to talk to you. Which they will in a moment, but only if they behave." He said the last bit loudly enough to make an impression. The kids got the hint and sat down at the table. "So," he said, his attention on Shelby. "Where did you say you are? It's a lousy connection. Must be the weather."

"Funny about the weather."

Static buzzed in his ear as a flash of lightning lit

the sky. He caught something out of the corner of his eye. Something on the porch. It was probably just a tree branch or maybe even the swing. But he headed toward the back door anyway. "What was that last thing?" he asked her. "I didn't hear you with that thunder."

"I said, funny about the weather."

"Why's that?"

"Well…"

Another brilliant flash of light arced across the sky. In that split second, he saw what had looked out of place on the porch. One very wet, very forlorn-looking woman. "What in hell?"

"Could you please just open the door?"

"What? Oh, man." He tried to keep the phone at his ear and unlock the door at the same time. It dawned on him that he could speak to her without the phone. All he had to do was usher her inside.

She hesitated before she stepped over the threshold and set her bag down. A big bead of water fell from the tip of her nose. "I'll get everything wet."

Gray grabbed her hand and pulled her in. "Who cares? You're drenched." He closed the door with his foot as he headed toward the guest bathroom. "Wait right there."

"I wasn't planning on going anywhere."

His mind reeled with the reasons she'd shown up again, soaked to the skin. Where was her car? Was she hurt? He jogged the last few feet to the bathroom and grabbed every towel in sight.

She had her shoes off by the time he made it back to the kitchen. He circled her with the largest towel. "What happened?"

"Car stopped."

"Stopped?"

She nodded as she took another towel from his hand and wrapped it around her wet hair. "On Mesquite Drive."

"That's over a mile from here."

"I know."

"Why didn't you call me?"

"I did. Over and over again."

Gray shot a glare at Jem, who sat hunched over the salt and pepper shakers at the table.

"Sorry, Shelby." The little boy looked like he was about to burst into tears.

"It's all right, Jem. But next time, leave the phone alone, okay?"

Jem nodded.

Gray turned to Shelby, and while she dried her hair, he got busy with the rest of her. He pulled the towel tighter, and she stumbled toward him.

SHELBY FROZE as her body touched his. The shock of instant awareness shook her with the power of the storm outside. His heat warmed her, his scent beckoned. She'd only been gone a few hours. How could this be?

He leaned toward her to kiss her, and her eyes fluttered closed. A second later and she turned in his arms, sneezing once, twice, three times.

"Bless you!" Scout shouted.

She sniffed. "Thank you. Then she felt Gray's hands on her arms and his body against her back. He leaned in close, and she could feel his hot breath on her ear. "Bless you," he whispered.

She shivered, not from the cold. He rubbed her

arms in long strokes, and for several moments she allowed herself to be taken care of.

"Are we going to eat soon?" Scout sighed loudly. "I'm hungry."

Shelby stepped away from the cocoon of Gray's arms. "I'll go get changed, then come help with dinner."

Gray turned her toward him. "I'm in charge of dinner. You go soak in a warm tub. I'll make you a tea or something."

Shelby was about to argue with him. That he was so willing to take charge was just the teensiest bit uncomfortable. After all, she was Shelby the rescuer, right? Then she thought about him rubbing her dry, his strong arms holding her close. She decided she wouldn't say anything except thank-you.

IT WAS SCARY how at home Shelby felt as she slipped into the warm water. As though this was exactly where she belonged. Not Dallas, not Austin, but here, with dinosaurs littering the living room floor, plastic frogs in the soap dish and Gray fixing her tea.

She leaned back, letting the bath soothe away the problems of the Maxima's engine, the walk to the house. Soon she'd be dry and comfy in her T-shirt and jeans, eating a dinner that she hadn't cooked. It was lovely.

Of course, there was that one troubling aspect, but for now, she made an executive decision. She was going to relax and enjoy herself if it killed her.

THEY FINISHED DINNER much later than usual, and it didn't take long for the kids' eyelids to start drooping.

Amazingly, they uttered only token protests when Gray told them it was time for bed.

Shelby was tidying up the living room when he came downstairs.

"Hey, you." He grabbed the wet rag she'd been using to clean jelly stains off the coffee table. "You're supposed to be taking it easy."

She made a face. "Why? I got a little wet. I'm over it."

"Well, okay then. But you still don't have to clean."

She looked at the tossed pillows, the row of Barbies by the couch, the popcorn on the floor.

"It'll wait for tomorrow."

"It will, huh?"

He nodded, but that turned into a yawn. "Man, I don't know how you women do it. Staying home all day with the kids is hard work."

"Really?"

He tossed the rag onto the arm of the couch and slipped both hands around her waist. "Taking off on that little excursion gave you a smart mouth."

"It wasn't an excursion. I was trying to get to Dallas." She pushed his hands away. "You can't leave that wet rag there."

He didn't give in so easily. This time when he caught her, he brought her in tight against his chest. "But fate conspired against you, didn't it?"

Her breath caught. She'd had the same thought, standing in the rain, looking at the warm glow coming from the windows of the house. "Don't be ridiculous. If the auto club hadn't been a four-hour wait, I wouldn't be in this mess."

He scowled. "This mess? You offend me."

She laughed, but the sound died on her lips as his face drew closer. "Gray." She gave a small jerk. Not enough to free herself, but he readily let her go.

He drove a hand through his hair. "I'm sorry, Shelby. I don't meant to push you. I just… I'm glad you're back. And not because I need help with the kids."

She believed him. He hadn't once asked for her help during dinner. In fact, he'd insisted she stay in her room and relax. Sure, the burgers were lopsided, the buns too toasted, but he'd handled everything by himself. Something that both disturbed and comforted her. She wanted to be needed, but she was glad he wanted her there even if he didn't need her.

Okay. So now she knew she needed to find a therapist in Austin.

"You're tired," she said, "and you don't need to entertain me."

He opened his mouth, a protest brewing in his gaze.

"Besides, I'm tired, too."

While he didn't seem happy, he didn't argue. "Fair enough."

"Go on upstairs," she said. "I'll be turning in soon."

"You aren't planning on doing anything more down here?" He started to shake his head. "Because—"

"Nope. I'm not. I just want to make a couple of phone calls. So go. Get out of here."

"It's only ten, you know," he said. "My bedtime isn't usually until at least ten-thirty."

She faked a yawn. He was incapable of not yawning in response. "You were saying?"

He gave in. "Fine. I'm going to bed. See if I care."

She went to pick up the wet rag, but his hand caught her arm. She turned to face him.

"You'll be here when I wake up, right?"

She didn't say anything for a long moment. "Yes. I'll be here."

"Good." He drew the back of his fingers down her cheek. "Sleep well."

She waited until he'd disappeared down the hall before she tried to move. Her legs wobbled, and her head hurt from the emotions welling inside. There was no doubt Gray had been genuinely glad to have her back. And when he said it had nothing to do with the kids, her heart had thumped so hard in her chest she thought she might burst.

She'd lied. No way was she going to get to sleep anytime soon. Not when she was fired up like this. What she did need, however, was time alone.

She made her way to the kitchen, lost in the dream that there was a future for her and Gray. Of course she knew he wasn't *that* happy to see her again. But still…

A glass of wine was in order, and just as she'd pulled the bottle from the fridge, the phone rang. Shelby grabbed it before it rang twice. "Hello?"

"Is this Shelby?"

"Yes," she said, recognizing the voice immediately. "How are you, Mr. Lattimer?"

"I'm fine. Just fine. Still can't get over those hors d'oeuvres of yours. I told them back at the test kitchen. You wouldn't happen to be looking for work, would you?"

"No, but thank you."

"I thought I'd try. Will you at least do me a favor?"

"If I can."

"Bring some of those delicious canapés to a little dinner I'm throwing Saturday night."

She hesitated. If all went well she'd still be here. But she doubted Gray wanted her to butt into his work. "I'll have to talk to Gray. If I can't make it, I'll send along a few things with him."

"You tell that husband of yours I insist. This is a family dinner."

"My husband?"

"He said you'd be there, so no changing your mind now. I just wanted to make sure y'all knew how to get here. You got a pen?"

Shelby got the notepad from the counter and poised her pencil. "Go ahead."

As Lattimer rattled off the directions, her mind spun a mile a minute. Her husband? What was that about? Had Gray tried to keep her here so he could make a good impression on his future boss? Was that what this whole thing was about?

CHAPTER THIRTEEN

"UNCLE GRAY, do you like Ariel or Belle better?"

Gray had no idea what Scout was talking about. "Ariel, definitely."

"Me, too." She turned to finish watching her cartoon.

She and Jem had been in the same position for the last hour—on their stomachs, heads held up by both arms, feet wagging behind them. He'd have cramped a long time ago, but they seemed very happy. In fact, nothing else had kept their attention like this movie.

He looked at the newspaper in his lap, but the thought of reading didn't appeal to him. He wanted to talk to Shelby.

After putting the paper on the floor, he headed for the kitchen. He found her checking on a coffee cake in the oven. "Can I help?"

"What? Oh, no. I've got it. This just needs to bake for another half hour, that's all." She wiped her hands on the towel she'd grabbed from the counter. "Gray, an odd thing happened last night after you went to bed."

"What?" He got the orange juice pitcher out of the fridge, poured himself a glass, then leaned against the counter.

"Mr. Lattimer called."

"Oh?"

"He wants us to come to dinner on Saturday."

He gave her his full attention. She seemed a little jumpy, maybe even impatient. Odd behavior for her. "Really?"

"He said you knew about it."

"Not exactly. He said something about getting together as he was leaving. That's all."

"I have the directions to his house. He asked me to bring some of the hors d'oeuvres I made the other day."

"Great. I take it you told him we'd go?"

She shook her head, her gaze staying carefully focused on him. "I told him I'd check with you. Gray, where did he get the idea we were married?"

Oh, man, he should have taken care of that. Damn. He'd forgotten all about it. He met her measured look sheepishly. "He sort of jumped to that conclusion while he was here, and I meant to correct it. But I..." He shrugged. "Did you straighten him out?"

"No," she said. "I didn't want to say anything to embarrass you."

Her tone of voice surprised him, as if she were disappointed. Maybe even angry. "Wait. I didn't intentionally lead him on, if that's what you're thinking."

"I didn't say that."

He shook his head. "He made that mistake when he was here. Just before he got in his car. I should have corrected him."

"Okay." She lifted a shoulder.

He frowned. "All Lattimer did was talk about family. How important it was to him. I guess I didn't want to let him know that I was an imposter."

"You weren't—aren't. You have a family."

"Not the kind he's talking about."

"Good thing I came back, then."

Her gaze skittered away, and he finally understood what had her upset. "You think that's why I wanted you to stay? Why I was so glad to see you?"

When she didn't answer, he said, "I swear to you, Shelby, I'd forgotten all about this. It's just a misunderstanding. I'll call him right now and straighten the whole thing out."

"You don't have to do that."

"Of course I do."

She looked away, then at him, her expression even more inscrutable. "We could wait until after he hires you."

Relief hit when he saw the mischief in her eyes. "That opens up a whole new can of worms."

"Right. Of course. We should just tell him."

He nodded again as he finished his juice. "On the other hand…"

"I suppose we could pretend."

"But if we do, how will I explain it later? When you're gone. When Ben and Ellen come back for the kids."

She frowned. "Oh, that."

"Yeah."

She stuck her left hand in her jeans pocket. God, she looked good enough to eat.

"I suppose we could do what they did in that movie."

"What movie?"

She shrugged. "I don't remember the name of it. That girl from 'Friends' was in it."

"Nope. Doesn't ring a bell."

"She needed to have a boyfriend for some reason

I don't remember. So she hired this guy and they acted all lovey-dovey at first. But then they staged a fight.''

"Well…" he said.

"It was just an idea," she said.

He thought about the scenario. Shelby and him together, acting like husband and wife. Then she disappears and he tells Lattimer what? That she left him? That she vanished?

"What are you thinking?" she asked. "You look like you've figured it out."

"I don't know. But Lattimer, he seemed like a real sympathetic kind of guy, right?"

"I guess."

"No, really. Didn't he seem like the kind of guy that would go the extra mile for someone in trouble?"

"Okay. Sure."

"So if he saw that I was crazy in love with you, and then I told him you left me, he wouldn't get mad. Not at me."

"Gee, thanks."

"You'll be in Austin. You won't see him again."

The humor that had lit her eyes when they started hatching the plot vanished in a blink.

"Never mind," he said. "We'll just tell him."

She turned, folded the dish towel. Set the stove timer. When she turned to him, she was smiling. But it didn't quite reach her eyes. "No. Let's do it your way. I agree. This way, he won't be embarrassed for getting it wrong, and he'll take care of you later."

"Are you sure?"

"No. Are you?"

He shook his head. "I'm not sure of anything any more." He caught her gaze and held it steady, willing her to fix things. To come up with the solution to a much more urgent problem.

"What?"

He let out a heavy breath. "I spoke to my sister yesterday."

"Kate, right?"

"Yeah. I told her about you."

"Oh?"

"And about our…situation."

Shelby poured herself the last of the orange juice and downed it as if it was whiskey.

"She thinks I'm growing up. Becoming a responsible adult."

"How do you feel about that?"

"I think she might be right. I know you won't believe me, but there have been times in the past when I was a real jerk."

"Ah, say it ain't so," she said, teasing him.

"It's true. I left women without so much as a phone call. And that's the best of it."

"But now?"

"Now, it seems, the pendulum has swung the other way."

"Imagine that."

"I know. Crazy."

"Then I guess I must be growing up, too."

"How do you mean?"

"Before this weekend, I'd never once kissed a man first."

"No?"

"I've certainly never instigated…you know… sex."

He smiled, but his engines were starting to rev. Big time.

"I've never been bold with any man in my life. Not once. I have a really close friend who got married recently. I was the maid of honor. And you know what? I'm only in one picture. One. You know why?"

"Tell me."

"Because I was in the bathroom for most of the night taking care of a very nice, very ill young lady whom I'd never met before. She got sick and upset, and I stayed with her. I missed the whole party."

He inched closer to her. "Yeah, I can see it. You're the first person I'd turn to if I was sick at a wedding."

She laughed, but it was hollow and ironic. "Not only am I not the bride, I'm not even the bridesmaid. I'm the sickroom attendant. If it isn't someone throwing up, it's someone crying over a broken engagement, or a lost job, or God knows what. It's so pathetic."

He inched closer still and slid his hand over until he found hers. "You're many things, Shelby Lord, but pathetic is not one of them."

She gave him a pleading look that made him want to hold her in his arms. He settled for squeezing her hand. "You've got a gift, you know."

"I do?"

He nodded. "You make people feel at ease around you. I've only known you a few days and I've told you more about myself than I've ever told anyone."

"Not to be rude or anything, but that's my point."

The hand thing wasn't cutting it. He turned to face her and grasped her upper arms, holding her still and forcing her to look right at him. "You're an incredible person. You're the most generous woman I've ever met. Not only that, but you're bright and successful and you're funny. You're beautiful and—''

''All right already. I said I'd go to Lattimer's with you—''

He leaned forward and kissed her. Kissed her as he'd been wanting to since yesterday. Kissed her hard, and pulled her to him. All his noble thoughts flew out the window. She was so soft against him it was a miracle. Her taste, her scent, everything about her excited him to fever pitch. Even though he knew he shouldn't, he pressed up against her, letting her feel what she was doing to him.

Her gasp told him she understood that he wasn't kidding. He took advantage of her open mouth and slipped his tongue inside, thrusting as he mimicked the act he burned to do. His hands moved down her back, and this time, she didn't jerk at the touch or try to move away. When he felt her soft palm against his neck, he almost lost it.

His mouth grew bold, insistent. His tongue took liberties, teasing and stroking until he made her moan. Finally, when he couldn't stand it another second, he moved his hand to the lush flesh of her breast. Even through her clothes he felt her heat, her plump nipple straining. He wanted to rip her clothes off, to enter her standing right here against the kitchen counter.

Then she touched him. Her small hand moved down from his belt buckle until her palm lay against his erection. It was a good thing he was in sturdy jeans or he probably would have burst through his seams.

He moved his hips, wanting more, wanting release. Her tongue against his taunted him, driving him closer and closer to the edge.

She squeezed him, and he cried out. Then her hand disappeared. Her lips moved from his. Somehow, through his haze of excitement, he felt her pressing against his chest.

"Gray," she said, and he was vaguely aware that she'd said it over and over.

He stopped. Stepped away. "Oh, my God."

"It's all right," she said.

"No, it isn't. I can't stand it. After all my talk about growing up, about acting respons—"

"Gray. Stop. Stop it. You're not being irresponsible. I'm a grown woman. I can make my own decisions."

"I know that."

"Do you?"

"Of course."

She let her gaze fall to his chest. "Sometimes I don't. I forget that I hold my destiny in my own hands. I keep waiting to get rescued. But that's crazy, because I don't have anything I need to be rescued from."

"What about dead engines?"

"Very funny."

The teasing glint left his eyes. "How about loneliness?"

She met his gaze, but only for a second.

"That's it, isn't it?"

"I'm not some old maid, sitting by the phone every night."

"I didn't say you were. I know without you telling me that you have a lot of friends. A lot of people who care about you. But I also know that you have a particular kind of love that isn't being used at all. And that from time to time, it feels empty."

Her gaze came back to his. Curious. Searching. "Do you feel that way, too?"

"It would be easier to say no. But I do. Not often. Just every once in a while."

"Oh?"

"Like today. If you had any brains at all you'd get away as soon as your car is running."

A small smile changed her face. Made it impossibly more beautiful. "Why is that?"

"Because I'm certifiable. I don't know what the hell I'm talking about, but that doesn't stop me from saying everything the second I think of it. You've put a spell on me, Shelby Lord. And I wish you'd take it off."

"If it was only that easy."

"You mean it's not?"

She laughed, but quietly. "I don't know what to make of all this. I'm acting completely out of character. From what you say, you're doing the same thing. The only conclusion I've come to is that we feel safe with each other. Safe because once I leave, that's that. I won't run into you accidentally at the market or the movies. You won't have to tell me you'll call when you know you won't. We're safe because we're strangers."

"I don't think of you as a stranger."

"We are."

"But—"

"We are, Gray, and you know it. This has been a moment, that's all. A strange interlude. Not the regularly scheduled program."

"That doesn't mean we can't see each other after—"

She put her hand on his mouth. "Don't. Please don't. I couldn't stand it if you lied to me now."

He took her hand away. "I'm not. Of course, I'm not saying we'd see each other all the time. I'll be starting a new job and it'll mean a lot of travel in the beginning and..." He stopped when he realized he was making things worse. The despair in her eyes shamed him. To his relief a bang came from the living room. "I guess the movie's over."

"We'd better go see if everything's all right."

"It's just that damn chair. They knock it over regularly."

"Still..."

"Shelby? I'm not lying."

"Let's leave it alone," she said, making it sound very definite. "No promises. No expectations."

"You're leaving when your car's ready, aren't you?"

She studied him for a long moment. He couldn't read her face, and it made him anxious. "I'll stay for Lattimer's dinner."

"And then?"

"I don't know."

He was probably foolish for pushing, but... "In the meantime, what are the rules?"

She lifted a brow. "Meaning?"

"Do I have to keep my hands to myself?"

She smiled shyly, but when her glance came up to meet his, there was nothing shy in her fiery eyes. He had a feeling it was going to be a great day.

AS IMPOSSIBLE as it seemed, the day had been longer and more tense than the day before. Yesterday, her

Maxima had been towed to a garage, whose charming mechanic couldn't even look at it until today.

That wasn't totally awful. In fact, whiling away the afternoon had helped her make a few decisions. She, Gray and the kids had kept busy, playing mostly. It had been a relaxing time, and because they'd been with Jem and Scout, there hadn't been too many anxious moments for her. Gray had been a real gentleman, but that didn't mean he hadn't shown interest.

Gray had gone upstairs to put the kids to bed. She slowly put the pieces of a puzzle in the box. Her thoughts turned to him. Of course. She thought about their conversation this morning, and thought even more about the moments when they hadn't talked. Kissing him had been a fatal mistake. If she'd never touched him, this whole problem would have been nothing but idle curiosity. But it was a little late for that.

She'd never reacted this way to any man, but she'd realized something. The more he restrained himself, the more hot to trot she became. It was uncomfortable to think about, but she knew deep down it was true. What she'd said about them being safe was even more accurate than she'd known at the time. It was safe to be brazen with Gray because she knew the worst that would happen would be a private humiliation. But would it be a humiliation she could stand?

When push came to shove, did she have the self-confidence to take it all the way? Or was she just a big old wuss, so frightened of rejection she'd never even let herself get near the starting gate?

So, what was she going to do about it? Run away? Jump his bones? Stay and do nothing?

She went to the guest bedroom and got her phone

out of her purse. She speed-dialed Abby Maitland's number.

"Shelby. What a nice surprise."

"I need some help."

"What is it?" Abby asked, her voice immediately concerned.

"I'm not sick or anything. I just need your opinion."

"Okay."

She took a deep breath. "Should I or should I not seduce the man I'm staying with?"

There was an awfully long silence. Then, "Pardon?"

"I'm in a great big house in Blue Point, Texas, with the hottest guy since George Clooney, and I think he wants me. The thing is, I don't know if I'm ready for this. Did I tell you he's gorgeous? And funny? And so out of my league I'm getting sick just talking about it?"

Abby laughed. "Slow down. Tell me what's going on."

"I'm here until Sunday. Then I'll never see him again. So it's safe, you see? I should do it, shouldn't I? I mean, it's not really like me, but it could be. If I were someone else."

"Okay. He's obviously turned your mind to mush and taken away all your good sense, so I'm leaning toward yes."

"Really?"

"But only if you feel perfectly safe. And I don't just mean using a condom."

"Safe as in if he's an ax murderer?"

"That, too. But what I mean is that you're not signing up for a whole heap of heartache. You're not the kind of woman who can separate sex and love.''

"Sure, I am.''

"No. You're not. Trust me on this. I've known you forever and I'm not the one who's been bamboozled by a gorgeous stranger. If you make love with him, something's going to shift. Now, do you think you can handle it? Leaving him, I mean?''

"Oh, damn.''

"That's what I thought.''

"But I want to seduce him. I'm tired of being a wuss and a coward.''

"Then ignore me. But, hon, if you didn't want to hear the truth, you would have called someone else.''

"Okay. Fine. I'll be perfect little Shelby. I won't color outside the lines or rock the boat or do anything that could possibly come back to kick me in the butt.''

"Shelby, I didn't say that. All I said was that you need to make the decision knowing all the facts. And the fact is, you can't love 'em and leave 'em. You love 'em and keep on loving them forever. Even when they don't love you back.''

Shelby's heart thudded against her chest as she sat on the bed. All the starch was seeping out of her as Abby's words hit home. It was true. She'd probably pay a dreadful price. Especially when she went back to the diner and watched all her friends with their new spouses. She'd felt alone before she left Austin, and when she went back it would be a hundred times worse.

"Shelby?''

"Yeah? I'm here. Did I tell you about the fate thing?''

"The what?"

"Never mind. It's nothing."

"I hope it all works out."

"Me, too."

"Call me tomorrow, okay? Let me know how you are."

"Right. Thanks, kiddo."

"My pleasure."

Shelby hung up the phone, but she didn't put it away. Her mind raced as she tried to think of a friend who would counsel her differently. Who would tell her she could seduce him to her heart's content and there would be no repercussions. That the act itself would fill her with so much confidence she'd attract the love of her life the moment she got back to Austin.

But none of her friends were liars.

"Shelby?"

She turned toward the door. He was looking for her, and she had to make up her mind. It was now or never. If it didn't happen tonight, it wasn't going to. "I'll be right out."

As she headed down the hallway, she straightened her shoulders. Brushed her hair with her palm. Moistened her lips. *Oh, God.*

CHAPTER FOURTEEN

HE MET HER in the living room. She pushed her hair behind her shoulder, just a casual move, one she probably made ten times a day. For some reason, the gesture made him want to kiss her, but he held back. Once he started, he wasn't sure he would be able to stop.

"Are they asleep?"

"They are. But not without much complaining that I wasn't reading the story right."

"I think that was just a ploy to stay up later, don't you?"

"Actually, I think they missed you."

She grinned. "Cool."

He took her hand and led her to the couch. "You know, it occurs to me that if we're going to carry on this grand facade at Lattimer's, we need to do some serious talking."

"What do you mean?"

"I mean I have no idea if you have any nieces or nephews. Or a dog or a cat."

"Oh, right."

"So what do you say we tell each other all our secrets."

Shelby smiled. "We've been doing that for five days."

"Yeah, I suppose you're right. Okay, so instead we'll just fill each other in on our backgrounds."

"It's a deal."

As he sat, she released his hand. He hadn't wanted her to. Just touching her made him calmer. Which was ironic, because looking at her made him edgy as hell.

"Do you want something to drink?" she asked him.

"How about a soda?"

"Coming right up."

She headed for the kitchen, and the moment she was through the swinging doors, Gray was on his feet, headed for Ben's CD player. His brother certainly had eclectic taste. Billie Holliday, Led Zeppelin, Enya. But as soon as he found the Sinatra CD, he looked no further. A moment later, Old Blue Eyes was singing about the wee small hours of the morning, and Gray knew all was right with the world.

Shelby came back holding two glasses. He met her at the couch, and they settled down. Wisely, she chose to sit in the chair across from his perch on the couch. With her eyes closed, she listened to the music for a moment, then smiled at him. "Nice."

"You like him, too?"

"Oh, yes. He was my mother's favorite. I grew up listening to Sinatra from the Capitol years."

"Your mother. I gather you mean your adoptive mother, right?"

She nodded.

"So go on. Tell me."

"My father was a banker and my mother was active on a lot of charity boards. They kept us together. They gave us everything we could ever hope for. Really, I had a remarkable childhood. We swam all summer, went camping and fishing. There was always a lot of noise in the house, but good noise, you know?''

He nodded. ''Sure.''

''My folks are gone now. I miss them every day.''

''It must have been hard.''

''Well, *you* know. At least, you know how hard it is to lose a mother. But I'll tell you a secret. I still talk to her from time to time. She's a hell of a good listener.''

''Does she ever talk back?''

Shelby smiled enigmatically. ''Sometimes.''

''So if you find your birth mother, what then? What do you want from her?''

''I want to talk to her. See if she's the reason for my red hair. Ask about our birth father. But mostly, I think I'd thank her.''

''Interesting attitude.''

''She must have loved us very much to make such a sacrifice.''

''What if it's not that way?''

Shelby shrugged. ''I think it is. Because I believe strongly that we're affected by nature more than nurture. You should see my family, Gray. Lana is so sweet. She owns a baby shop in Austin.''

Shelby rose, tucked her feet under her in what Gray was beginning to see was her favorite position.

''She just got married, and her husband already has a child that Lana loves as if he were her own.''

As she spoke, her face changed. He saw the longing there. She wanted her own family so badly. That's undoubtedly why she'd stayed here. She couldn't bear to see an oaf like him take care of such young kids. Whatever her reason, he was grateful.

"Michael found someone, too," she continued. "His secretary. They have a baby. In fact, she was pregnant when they eloped."

"I suppose Garrett is about to become a father, too?"

"Oh, no. Not Garrett. He's a really good guy, I mean it. And he'd make a wonderful father. But things have been pretty rough on him lately. I don't think he'd be interested in a woman right now, let alone a child."

Gray got up after grabbing his empty glass. "More soda?"

"No, thanks. I'm fine."

He walked past her toward the kitchen, and almost against his will his hand brushed her arm. He stopped with his fingers on her shoulder. His legs simply refused to work. It was as if touching her had changed the very air around them. He felt restless, charged, like he'd walked into the middle of a lightning storm.

She raised her hand, so soft it was like a child's, and put it atop his. He forgot to breathe. To think. All he knew how to do was want her.

"Gray, do me a favor. Hold off on that drink a minute and come sit down."

It was a Herculean effort to take his hand away. To walk that short walk to the couch. But he did it. For her.

"I've made a decision. One I think you'll be glad to hear."

"What's that?" he asked, surprised at the tension in his gut. She was going to leave. That's what she was going to tell him. She wasn't going to pretend to be his wife. Of course not. That was a damn foolish thing to—

"I've decided not to seduce you."

He burst out laughing. "You decided *what?*"

"It's not funny. So please stop laughing."

He cleared his throat in an attempt to obey, but the way she'd said it was classic. She'd been completely earnest, not at all self-conscious. With her feet peeking out at the side of the chair cushion, she couldn't have looked more innocent if she'd worn pigtails and carried a lollipop.

"I mean it," she repeated, and he could see she was irked.

"No, no. Of course you did. I'm sorry for laughing. I just didn't expect you to say that."

"Oh. Well, then, I suppose it's okay."

He nodded as if everything was peachy keen. "Want to tell me why?"

She looked past him to the CD player on the entertainment-center shelf. Sinatra was singing about being young at heart. When Shelby turned his way again, she seemed determined, yet there was that telltale hint of pink on her cheeks. "I'm not the love 'em and leave 'em type."

He almost laughed again. With a supreme effort he kept his amusement to himself. "No?"

"No. I wanted to be. I really did. But I don't think I can be."

"What do you mean you wanted to be?"

"Like I said. I was going to seduce you. Although I have to confess, you haven't always been very cooperative about it."

"I'm not sure I agree with that."

"But it turned out to be the right thing, of course," she said, ignoring him.

"Of course."

"Let me get that soda now. I'm thirsty, too."

Confused, he watched her stand up, walk over to him with that delectable sway in her hips, take his glass and head for the kitchen. Just after she'd disappeared, he realized his mouth was hanging open.

This week had definitely been the strangest of his life. It was almost too much for him to believe that he hadn't swept Shelby off to a long night of wild sex. It was what he did best, after all. He'd let the opportunity slip through his fingers, and he'd never see it again.

What a jackass.

She came back with two full glasses and a bag of potato chips. After handing him his drink, she held up the bag. "Want some?"

He sure as hell did, but not chips. He wanted some of her. No. He wanted all of her. In his bed. Underneath his body, with that red hair of hers flared on the pillow. He wanted to sink inside her wet heat until one of them passed out. The desire that had been tormenting him since day one had just gone ballistic. His hand shook as he brought his soda to his lips.

Unmindful of his dilemma, Shelby took her seat again, sipped some soda and smiled. The smile was short-lived however. "Are you all right?"

He managed a nod.

"Are you in pain?"

All he could do was roll his eyes.

"Do you need a doctor?" she asked, leaning forward anxiously. "Maybe you caught the same bug Jem had."

"No," he said, his voice a husky fake. "I just, uh, have a headache, that's all."

"Oh, no. I'll get you some aspirin."

He didn't stop her. Not that he needed the medicine, but he did need her to go away. He had to get a grip. It wouldn't do to jump on the lady moments after she'd confessed that she wasn't comfortable with a one-night stand. It could be misconstrued.

But damn it, if his brother had had a swimming pool like every other rancher in Texas, he'd have jumped in the deep end, clothes and all.

And Kate said reverse psychology was nonsense. Ha! He was a living, breathing testament. What a jackass! He lowered his head into his hands, moaning with the agony he deserved.

SHELBY FOUND the aspirin right next to the box of condoms. The reminder of her plan made her wince. Not because the plan had been a bad one, but because she'd fumbled it so thoroughly. It just went to prove that she was completely incompetent when it came to matters of the heart. Or of the bed.

She *knew* he wasn't lying about wanting to be with her. Nothing anyone could say or do would convince her otherwise. A smart woman would have made these few days into exactly what she wanted. It should have been a week of new experiences, of abandon, of pure pleasure. Instead, it had been awkward and frustrating. The worst part of it was the awful realization that she was getting exactly what she asked for, and it felt completely lousy!

She really, really wanted him. But Abby was right. It wasn't a want that could be sated with one night. She'd grown to like Gray Jackson. Maybe even more than like him.

She closed the bathroom cabinet with a bang and

hurried to the living room. But Gray wasn't there. Maybe the kitchen?

It was empty, too, and the back door was open. Shelby poured a small glass of water and ventured outside, her concern growing by the moment.

She found him sitting on the beautiful old-fashioned wooden porch swing. The view of the night sky was wonderful. The moon was full and looked so near she could see the Sea of Tranquility.

"Are you all right?" she asked.

"Yes. I'm fine. Thanks."

"I've brought your aspirin."

He patted the seat beside him. "Come sit down."

She did, wondering if it was the moon that had pulled him outside. After handing him the glass and the pills, she sat, completely aware that it was a mistake to be so close to him. They didn't touch, but they weren't even an arm's length apart.

Instead of swallowing the medicine, he put the pills and the water on the porch railing, then he turned to her and gave her a halfhearted grin.

"Why didn't you…?"

"What ails me can't be cured by aspirin," he said.

"Oh?"

He shook his head.

"Want to tell me?"

His brows went up as he gave her a very emphatic, "No."

"Okay."

She pushed with her foot, and the rocker did its job, silently moving them back and forth in the cool night air. She wished she could see more of the porch. She hadn't really looked during the downpour. There was a barbecue pit that looked big enough to handle a whole cow. A built-in bar. A round table with an umbrella. A great porch for a family. Perfect for summer evenings, and not half bad for a clear winter night, either.

"It's your turn," she said.

He gave her a wary look.

"Come on out with it, Jackson. I know you've had a wild life, but I'm old enough to take it."

His grin widened. "Are you, now?"

"Oh, yeah. Nothing shocks me anymore. I've heard it all."

"You're lying."

"Yeah, I know. But it sounded good, didn't it?"

His low chuckle made her shiver.

"The awful truth is, Ms. Lord, that my life isn't all that shocking. In fact, when you put the whole of it together it doesn't amount to very much."

"Don't say that."

"Why not? It's true. Even my own mother knew it."

"All mothers worry. It's their job. It doesn't mean she wasn't proud, too."

"Good try."

"So what do you think would make her proud?"

"That's easy. She'd have been thrilled if I'd only been like Ben."

"Not good enough. What exactly would need to be different?"

"A steady job with a future. A home. A family. A retirement plan, a healthy savings account."

"Hmm. That's interesting. But are you sure?"

"Why do you ask that?"

"Because I know what my mother wanted for me."

"Which was?"

"To be happy. To follow my dreams. To be kind and generous with my heart as well as my pocketbook. She wanted me to love and to be loved. And she wanted me to take risks, as long as I walked in knowing the score."

He didn't say anything. She crossed her arms against the cold, but it really wasn't bad. Mostly it was quiet, and for the first time since she'd been in Blue Point, she felt completely at peace.

Talking about her mother had made things clear in her mind. Whatever happened with Gray, it was important for her to trust her instincts. To follow her heart. She wasn't sure where that was going to lead, but when the journey was through she knew it would be something to remember. Something to look back on with a sweet sense of nostalgia.

She'd been teasing when she'd told Gray that her mother sometimes talked back. But in truth, she did. She just had.

"I play the saxophone," Gray said.

"Really?"

He nodded. "Not terribly well. But I used to love it."

"And?"

"And it's been a lot of years since I've picked that saxophone up."

"I never played an instrument, but I used to sing in the choir. That was nice."

"There were lots of nice things, weren't there?"

"Oh, yes."

They rocked some more. She stared at the moon. And then she felt his hand on hers. His fingers, so strong and sure, slid in between hers, and he gave her a gentle squeeze. She closed her eyes, concentrating on the feel of him. In years to come she'd fly back here on the wings of her memory, and she wanted to get it exactly right.

"I'm sorry, Shelby."

"For what?"

"For being such a jerk. I shouldn't have tried to keep you here. I shouldn't have kissed you, even though I enjoyed the hell out of it. I had no right to take you from your life just to make mine a little easier."

"I don't recall complaining."

"You wouldn't. You're not like that."

"I could have left the moment I knew this was a dead end."

"Yeah, but then you saw how inept I was with the twins."

She smiled. "They really had you there, didn't they?"

"Total capitulation on my part. All that was left was the victory party."

"Are you sorry I stayed?"

"No. I'm sorry you left yesterday."

Hope made her a little light-headed.

He looked at her, and the light from the moon made the determination on his face as clear as if he'd been under a spotlight. "Go home tomorrow, Shelby. Go home. I can take it from here."

Her heart beat a little faster. She had to swallow twice, but his words didn't crush her. If it was meant to be...

"But I'd like to call you, if I may. After I settle in a little more."

"I'd like that."

He sighed. "I'm glad. Because the thought of never

seeing you again isn't something I care to contemplate.''

"What about Lattimer?''

"I'm going to tell him it was a mistake. If it costs me the job, I'll get another.''

"It won't. He already sees how valuable you'll be to his company—what a fine man you are.''

He leaned over and kissed her on the cheek. "I envy your friends,'' he whispered. "And I'd like to be one of them.''

"You already are.''

He stayed close, his lips grazing her cheek, his warm breath touching her blush. She didn't think. She didn't try to figure it out. She just turned. Wouldn't you know, her lips and his met right in the middle. Fate.

CHAPTER FIFTEEN

IT WAS DIFFERENT this time. As if she'd never kissed him before. As if she'd never been kissed. He caressed her with his lips, savored her as if she was rare and exotic. His hand moved to her arm, but his touch was tentative. She parted her lips, and with that, everything changed again. Now confident, he slid his hand up to her shoulder.

As she melted into his arms, she knew exactly what she was doing and how much it was going to hurt to leave him. But it seemed absurd that she'd considered the alternative. Much better to be with Gray tonight and lose him than never to have been with him at all.

The swing rocked, and he shifted, but the position wasn't right. She wanted to be closer to him, to be free to stroke him everywhere and be stroked in return. She wanted him inside her.

He pulled away and stood in front of her, holding out his hand. She took it, and he led her inside. They walked through the familiar kitchen to the hallway, his hand strong and sure, her mind at peace, even though the closer they got to his bedroom, the harder her heart pounded. He opened his door, then paused to let her go in first. After she'd crossed the threshold, he stepped to her side and closed the door.

She'd only seen the room once, and for just a moment. It wasn't terribly large, but there was plenty of room for the king-size bed, the dark wooden armoire and the desk in the corner. But nothing in the bedroom was more impressive than the moonlight streaming in from the big bay windows.

Gray reached for the light switch, and she held her breath. He looked at her, then pulled his hand back. She knew, with absolute certainty, that he'd demurred out of courtesy, not because he didn't want to see.

The silver glow from the moon wouldn't hide her sudden grateful tears. His consideration…

He came up behind her and put his hands on her shoulders, right at the base of her neck. Pressing his body against her back, she could feel his heat, his readiness. His acceptance. Then his warm breath caught her just below her ear, and she tilted her head so he had room to move. Hot kisses were her reward, a nip of her ear, more kisses. "I've never wanted anything more," he whispered, "than to be inside you."

She quivered, squeezed her legs together, reached back so she touched his sides with her palms. He kissed her again, then he turned her around. The light hit him perfectly so she could see the details of his face. His eyes, so hungry. His little smile, as if he was in on something secret and special.

"I can't believe you're here."

"I can't believe it, either. But now that I am here…" She raised a coy eyebrow.

He laughed, and it was a gorgeous sound. Deep and rich and full of life. But he got the point. His hands went to the bottom of his T-shirt, and he pulled it up and off, tossing it to the floor behind him. "Your turn."

Her fingers went to the bottom of her shirt, but once there, she froze. She wished there was no moon. No way he would see the extent of her scarring. He was so perfect. Not a flaw on his body. The old fear rose in her like a tidal wave. She couldn't.

His hands touched hers, moving them to her sides. Then he took over. He caught her gaze and held it as he lifted the shirt slowly. His smile told her not to worry, but she couldn't help it.

His gaze moved down to her breasts. She didn't have to look to see that her nipples were visibly hard. He shook his head as if he couldn't quite believe she was standing there. Then he looked up. "May I?"

She nodded, feeling very brave. He undid the front clasp a second later, then paused. After a long breath, he peeled the material back. He leaned over and kissed her, then gently pushed her straps off her shoulders. The bra fell while he moved closer and wrapped his arms around her.

Flesh against flesh. Her breasts pressed against his chest, and when he moved, she gasped at the sensation of his hard muscle and the rasp of hair. He captured her mouth and kissed her. No longer tentative, he took her breath away with the power of his lips, his tongue. He thrust into her, pulled back, thrust again, a prelude to what was coming. She held on to him, feeling the tension in his shoulders, savoring her own power as the hard evidence of his arousal urged her to finish undressing.

He must have been thinking the same thing. The kiss abruptly ended and he stepped back, undoing the buttons of his Levi's. She concentrated on her jeans, kicking off her shoes then stripping herself bare. She held her breath as she straightened her shoulders, ready to face him, to be seen.

He straightened at the same time. His body stunned her with its sculpted beauty. Broad shoulders, muscled chest and abs. His erection was as hard and perfect as the rest of him. Impossibly perfect.

"You're beautiful," he whispered.

"You are."

"Shelby, look at me."

"I am. That's the problem."

He touched her under her chin until her gaze met his. "I have news for you, kiddo." His voice was as gentle as a caress. His eyes kind and something more. Something she couldn't identify. "I'm not a very nice person."

"Excuse me?"

"I said, I'm not a particularly nice guy. In fact, I'm more or less a selfish bastard. Have been all my life."

"But—"

He touched his fingers to her lips.

"The point to this confession is that I'm not doing this out of mercy." He took her hand in his, pulling it gently toward his erection.

When she grasped him, he gasped as if she'd hurt him. But she knew she hadn't. It was just such intense pleasure that it was hard to bear.

"Any questions?"

She had to smile. The evidence was pretty overwhelming. What if she decided, just for tonight, that she *was* beautiful? That he *did* want her desperately? Would the world stop turning? Would she be punished?

If she was, then so be it. Because tonight she was going to make love. Tonight she was going to let her body accept pleasure. She was going to trust.

She began to stroke him all the way up and down, loving the feel of the soft skin covering his hard length. Soon he would be inside her. They would join together to be one being. Then she remembered. "I have a condom in my room," she whispered.

He bent down, dislodging her hand. He grabbed his jeans and pulled a silver packet from the pocket and handed it to her. "Ta da."

It was the same brand as the condom she'd swiped from the medicine cabinet. He must have had the same idea. "Why, Mr. Jackson. I do believe you had designs on me."

"Who, me?"

She nodded.

"Okay. You're right. Will you do the honors?"

She grinned. "Oh, boy. I've never done this before." She tore open the packet and admired the elegant simplicity of the device. She reached for him again, and his yelp told her she'd gotten a little too enthusiastic. "Sorry."

"It's okay. Just remember, it's attached."

She grinned as she rolled the condom down. "Pretty good for a first time, eh? Well, except for that little mistake."

"Excellent."

"I'm a fast learner," she said. "Which is good, because tonight, you need to teach me."

He gave her one cocked brow, kissed her hard on the lips. Then in one swift move she was suddenly in his arms, on the bed, her head on the pillow, her arms at her sides. He bent over her, kissing her again, chasing away all coherent thought. She ached for him. Physically. Emotionally. But she had to be patient.

He abandoned her mouth and moved his kisses to her chin, then down her neck. She closed her eyes as he licked her, tasted her, teased her inch by inch, lower and lower. He paused at her breasts, taking her heavy nipples into his mouth and sucking on them hard, making her squirm. No longer able to lie still, she raised her hands to his shoulders, but as he moved lower she tensed. She didn't want to. But there were so many years of believing she was ugly. It wasn't something she could change overnight.

Her hand went to her waist, covering up the scar tissue there. He hesitated, then lifted her hand away. Gently, he kissed her palm. And then he bent his head and kissed her right there. Right where she'd felt so damaged, so unworthy. He kissed her again and again. She closed her eyes, hardly believing this was happening. It was better than her dreams had even dared.

Her eyes opened at her next thought, and she leaned forward, looking between their bodies. She relaxed as she saw his erection was as proud as ever.

He didn't notice the move. He was too busy trailing his lips down her tummy. He blew a soft stream of warm air into her belly button, which tickled and made her laugh. But her laughter ceased as his voyage continued, as he nudged her legs apart. His fingers touched the patch of hair that partly hid her moist center. He stroked her nether lips, starting a quiver inside her from her toes all the way up. When he parted those lips and blew another stream of warm air, she cried out with the sweet agony of her desire.

She reached for him, but he had plans of his own. He caressed her with his mouth, his tongue, setting her afire. She squirmed under him, her breath coming in great gasps as the tension in her body increased. This was all new to her. She had no idea it could be this incredible.

He continued to work his magic until her hands fisted around the blanket as she strained for release. Every muscle in her body tensed, and she couldn't breathe at all.

He increased the pressure, teasing her harder, harder, until she exploded with a climax that made the world disappear. Trembling and twitching as little earthquakes shook her body, she pulled at him, willed him to move up so she could share this moment.

He obeyed. And as he moved, his knees pushed her legs apart and up. Finally, he was above her, his gaze locked on hers. At that moment, he slipped inside her, reawakening the sensations that had calmed only seconds before.

She expected pain. But there was nothing like that. Just the incredible sensation of being full where she'd been empty. Complete.

After an infinite pause, he thrust into her all the way. She climaxed again, her muscles squeezing him, her head thrashing on the pillow. He stilled her with a kiss as he pulled out almost all the way, then in again, so powerfully she wanted to weep.

The kiss ended, but not their connection. He stared at her as he found his rhythm, as her hips moved to meet his in a dance she'd never known before. His gaze never let her go, so deep that she felt he was inside her mind as well as her body.

It was all new, intense, so feral. She wanted him deeper even though she knew she couldn't take any more. Her hands raked his back as he thrust again and again, as the tempo quickened, as his climax neared.

His face contorted as if with pain, and the muscles of his neck grew taut as he reared his head. With a low, animal growl, he came inside her. Never before had anything felt so right. It was as if they were melting into one being, one heart, one cry.

And then he laughed. A joyous bark of triumph. His gaze went to hers, and she saw her pleasure in his eyes, in his smile. He kissed her once more, and all the while her body was still squeezing him, still trembling.

"Shelby," he whispered. "Wow."

"I know. Can you believe it? Pretty damn good for a first time, huh?"

He laughed again. "I think you've summed up my feelings quite well."

She grinned. "We'll probably have to do it again, just to make sure it wasn't a fluke."

"Oh, baby, I'm right there. Only, I need a little time to recover."

"Okay. How about ten minutes?"

He moaned as he rolled over, slipping out of her, making her want him in her again the next second.

He settled next to her, his head on her pillow. Then he took the blanket and threw it over both of them. His hand rested on her stomach as his breathing slowed.

Shelby felt bathed in voluptuousness. In utter

bliss. She never wanted to leave this bed, this man.
A dark thought sprang up, but she chased it away,
refusing to let yesterday or tomorrow steal any of
today's joy.

He stroked her belly as if she were his pet, and
she damn near purred. There was no question in her
mind that this was meant to happen. It was fate, all
right.

Her eyes fluttered closed as she drifted near sleep.
She couldn't help thinking that fate had more in store
for her and Gray. How, she wasn't sure. She was
going home. Not tomorrow morning. No, she was
determined to be there with him at Lattimer's dinner.
To help him attain his dream. But Sunday, she'd
head on back to Austin.

His breathing had slowed and deepened. She
wanted to ask him if he thought it was as wonderful
as she did. But it wasn't exactly the kind of thing
she could just blurt out. Turning toward him, she
realized she didn't have to ask. He lay with his eyes
closed and the sweetest smile on his face. She
doubted very much he even knew he was smiling.
But she knew. Oh, my.

GRAY WOKE UP. The first thing he did was turn to
look at Shelby. God, she was beautiful. If he had a
brain in his head, he'd never let her go. She'd be an
incredible wife. The problem was, what kind of husband would he be? The answer was obvious. He'd
be lousy. His mother had been right to worry about
him. He'd never taken responsibility for anything in
his life. He'd let the wind lead him, always following
the lure of something better around the bend.

But a husband had to be there. All the time. And

if they had children? Hell, a father had to place the child's welfare above his own. That was one tall order for a selfish bastard like him. Even now, lying next to this incredible woman, all he could think of was himself. Him, him, him.

He turned on his side, facing Shelby. Her eyes were closed and her breathing deep and even. She looked wonderful. Everything about her was right. Her curves. He'd never been with a woman who was so easy to touch, so soft. He'd never been with a real redhead before, either.

And he'd never been with anyone so unselfish. That was Shelby, wasn't it? Completely unselfish. She'd stayed for him, for the kids. Taken time from her own life to help a stranger. And what had he done in return? Against his better judgment, he'd taken her to his bed. He'd been so damned determined to take the high road, and he'd cracked like a dry twig the moment she'd kissed him.

He deserved to be horsewhipped. He certainly didn't deserve the wonderful creature beside him.

She stirred, and he kept very still. When she settled once more, he breathed again and looked at the clock. It was just after midnight. He felt as if it should have been much later. He wished she wasn't asleep.

"Gray?"

He started, turning to her again. "Did I wake you?"

She shook her head, but he didn't believe her. With those half-closed eyes and those catlike stretches, he knew she was still mostly asleep.

"Can I get you something?"

Again, she shook her head. "I wish you could do this for me, but you can't."

"Oh, right."

She sat up, letting the blanket fall to her waist. The instant he saw her he got excited again. Too excited. What was it about her?

He watched as she walked to the bathroom, her naked body silver in the moonlight. The soft sway of her hair and her hips turned up the voltage running through him. As she closed the door he sat up, and it occurred to him that he'd been holding back with her because she wasn't a one-night kind of woman. He hadn't wanted to put her in a situation where she'd regret being with him. So why was it that *he* was the one who didn't want her to leave? He was the one filled with regret—not that they'd made love, but that he wanted to make love again. And again.

This was unprecedented. Come morning, most mornings, he was history. Always had been. Not literally, sometimes, but emotionally every time. He disconnected. Moved on. Now he understood that he'd never been connected to begin with.

Shelby had changed that. He wanted more. Not marriage, nothing that extreme, but he wanted to be with her again. No mistake about that.

She had become the ultimate distraction. He'd barely thought about the job. A chill ran through him. Was that what this was about? An excuse to fail at this new life?

He needed this job, damn it, and not because of his mother or Shelby. He needed to learn to trust himself. He needed a place to call home. A future.

The bathroom door opened, and she walked

slowly to the bed. Her smile made his chest constrict. Several other things constricted, too, but he thought it best to ignore them for now. He moved the blankets, and she crawled in next to him.

"Hi."

"Hi, back."

She kissed him on the nose. "I fell asleep. I didn't mean to."

"That's okay. You were really pretty."

"Ha. I probably drooled or something."

"Nope. You were just perfect."

She sighed as she brought the covers to her armpits. "I'm not terribly sleepy right now."

"No?"

She shook her head.

"What do you think we should do?" he asked.

"Well, from that tent you've made of the blanket, I have an idea what you think we should do."

"So much for subtlety."

"Yeah."

She hunkered down on the bed, and he followed suit, moving the blanket so that he could feel her body. Her soft warmth. His hand went to her stomach again, and he rubbed small circles. But when he touched her scar, she flinched.

He sighed, shook his head. "Shelby, Shelby." He leaned down and kissed her where his hand had been.

"It's just that—"

He looked up at her. "Get over it."

"I just can't believe I deserve so much joy."

"You deserve all this and more."

"Do I really?" she asked so quietly he barely heard her.

"Oh, yes." He moved up her body so his lips were inches from hers. "All that and the moon," he whispered with a kiss.

She kissed him back.

Then, *heaven*.

CHAPTER SIXTEEN

SHE OPENED HER EYES to the first hint of daylight. And Gray. It was wonderful looking at him like this, when he couldn't see her. She took her time, blessing the light that fell across his face.

He was so beautiful. Like no one else she'd ever known. Perfect, but in his own way. Even now, with his hair tousled, in need of a shave, he made her heart flutter. That he was so sweet inside was even more remarkable.

She wanted—

Oh, God, she wanted him. Forever. She wanted to wake up next to him every day for the rest of her life. It came as no surprise. In fact, she'd already known on some level, but the plain bald truth was that she was in love with him.

For so long now she'd watched her closest friends fall in love and she'd wished and wished that it could happen to her. She should have been more specific.

If only he wasn't so set on getting the job with Lattimer. If only she didn't love her diner so much, and her life in Austin. If only he wanted the kind of committed relationship she was looking for.

If only...

She reached over and gently moved a lock of his hair. Even a touch as innocent as that had her wanting him in a way she'd never understood before. It was as if her body had been made complete. And when she left, as she had to, there would be an empty space inside her forever.

It wasn't fair, and it wasn't fun. And—oh, she'd promised herself she wasn't going to do this! Her eyes had been open. She'd walked in on her own two feet. She'd understood from the first that leaving him was going to be hard.

What she hadn't realized was that it felt as though it might kill her.

"What's wrong?"

She jerked in surprise. "You're asleep."

"Oh. Then I must be dreaming, right?"

She nodded.

He grinned. "Some dream. Don't wake me."

"Gray?"

"Hmm?"

"Nothing."

His eyes widened, and he looked awake. "What?"

She couldn't tell him. It wasn't fair. And yet the desire was so great it made her dizzy.

He glanced at the clock. "It's early still."

"I know. Go back to sleep."

"I don't want to."

"You should. You need to be on your toes tonight."

His eyes closed with a grimace. "Oh, that."

"Yeah, that."

He moved his legs so they touched hers, but stopped himself from moving his upper body. "You know what?"

"Hmm?"

"I'm going to brush my teeth."

"Oh, good idea."

"You do understand why I'm going to brush my teeth, don't you?"

"So you'll taste minty fresh?"

He threw the covers back and got up, showing her that he wasn't kidding about his designs on her. Then he scurried to the bathroom while she enjoyed the view of his incredible behind. As soon as the door closed, her thoughts went back to her decision. Tell him? What would be the worst thing that could happen?

He'd tell her he didn't feel the same way. That he'd never meant to hurt her. That they'd always be friends.

She shuddered. Okay, so what was the best that could happen? He'd tell her he loved her right back. That he'd move heaven and earth to be with her, and surely there was a great opportunity just waiting for him in Austin. He'd tell her he would never let her go.

There was a chance, right? A small one, but hey, miracles happened all the time. People found their soul mates. Love could be real and last for a lifetime.

He opened the door, and she made up her mind as he hurried back to bed. She was going to take the biggest risk of all.

He got under the covers with a great deal of kicking sheets and punching pillows. She needed to go brush her teeth, too, but first, she wanted to say this—before she lost her nerve.

"You know what occurred to me?" he asked.

"What?" she said, her heart swelling with hope that it was the same thing that had occurred to her.

"I need someone to sit for the kids tonight."

A stab of disappointment hit her right where it hurt most. He wasn't thinking about her at all. And why should he? "I have the name of a woman who's taken care of them before."

"How?"

"I met her at the mall the day I left."

His brows furrowed, and he stared in silence for a moment. He didn't have to verbalize what he was thinking. She should have given him the information immediately. Then his expression relaxed, and he leaned forward and kissed her. "You're the best."

"I need to go smell minty fresh, too. Then we can discuss my wonderfulness some more."

His laughter followed her across the carpet. She closed the door behind her and braced herself against the cold wood. She couldn't tell him. It wouldn't be fair.

Besides, she already knew the outcome.

THE BED WAS EMPTY when he awoke. The first thing he saw was the dip in the pillow where she'd slept. Shower. She was probably in the shower. Maybe she'd like company. He tossed the covers aside and headed across the carpet, amazed that he felt as good as he did. His night hadn't exactly been one of uninterrupted sleep. Not that he was complaining. Every time he woke up, Shelby had been there, and one thing had led to the other. Three times. Some people might even say four. But definitely three.

The bathroom door was slightly ajar. He didn't hear the water running, but that didn't mean she wasn't in there. He tapped lightly, and when he got no response he pushed the door open. Empty. Was she gone? Had she left without saying goodbye?

He turned abruptly and headed for the bedroom window. There was her car, right where the mechanic had left it yesterday. Okay. She was still here. But she wouldn't be soon, would she? As he headed back to the bathroom he noticed his rapid pulse, his shallow breathing. She'd scared him. The thought of her leaving had been terrible.

How could it be? He hadn't known her long enough to have this kind of reaction. It wasn't like him at all. He got his toothbrush and began the morning rituals, but his mind was squarely on Shelby. She was great, sure, but love? Nah. Not him.

He knew exactly what was going on, but the awareness didn't lessen his anxiety. Shelby had come into his life just when he was about to become the man he should have been all along. The man his mother wouldn't have worried about. But the idea of changing like this had scared the hell out of him. Then Shelby had walked through his door.

A delectable distraction. She made it easy with her musical laughter, her sly humor and that damn red hair. He'd switched his focus immediately. His thoughts hadn't been on the job or his future. Just Shelby.

So what happened now? Just because he could identify the behavior didn't mean he could change it. The pull toward her was just as strong as ten minutes ago. The urge to hurry just as acute.

Maybe he should call Kate. Ask her. Or maybe he should stop thinking about Shelby. He turned on the water in the shower, let it heat up for a few seconds, then climbed in. It felt great. He put some shampoo on his hand and washed his hair. And he didn't think about Shelby even once. Well, this thought didn't count. If he'd thought of, say, last night. How she'd moved under him. How her face had looked when—

Stop. Jeez. Tonight. He needed to be on his toes tonight. Lattimer was a tough old guy, and he might smile and laugh, but Gray had seen how his keen eyes had missed nothing. If it hadn't been for Shelby the last time—

He stuck his head under the water and gave up. It was no use. He couldn't stop thinking about her. Proof positive of his theory. He'd be so wrapped up in thinking about Shelby that he'd screw up tonight. Then, conveniently, when he didn't get the job, he could blame her. A nice little scenario, one that would hold up over time.

So what was he supposed to do now? Ask her to leave? Ask her to stay? But if he asked her to stay and he did great with Lattimer, what then? She'd have to leave before he started the job, right? So would he use the excuse that Shelby was in Austin to weasel out of the job?

Damn it. He was no good at all this analytical bull. Never had been. He was a man of action. So what action was he supposed to take?

He sighed as he grabbed a washcloth. Today was going to be a doozy.

SHELBY closed her eyes as the porch swing rocked beneath her. It was different without the moon. Without Gray. The view was better. Of course that depended on what she was looking for. If it was beautiful scenery, then the daytime view won hands down. If she was looking for love...

She sighed. Love. What a concept. She hadn't ever imagined it this way. In her head, it was complete happiness. A coming together of two souls who had been incomplete without each other. A union made in heaven. Not this. This was at heart a tragedy. A woman loving a man who didn't love her back.

Why in hell couldn't she, for once, be the girl who gets the guy? Was she always going to be on the outside looking in? Was this ache in her heart going to haunt her forever?

Why had she come here in the first place? God's little sociology experiment? *Let's let her fall in love to see how that feels, but then let's take the love element away.* Ha, ha. Very funny.

It wasn't funny at all. It hurt, and it hurt bad.

She should go inside. The kids were undoubtedly up, and heaven knew what they'd gotten into. As she rose, she thought about Gray in bed. The feel of his thigh as it rested against hers. The image gave her goose bumps, and that weird little thing happened in her tummy. It felt like a thrill, as if her body was excited by him all on its own.

"Well, body," she said, "better get over it."

"Get over what?"

She whirled around at Gray's voice. She hadn't heard him at the door. "You scared me."

"I'm sorry. I didn't mean to."

"It's okay. Are the kids up yet?"

He nodded. "They're watching cartoons."

"Ah, then I'd better make breakfast." She tried to slip past him, but he caught her arm.

"Hey, wait."

She looked at him, only inches away. His clean-shaven face was as handsome as ever. More so now that she understood it so well. How his right brow was slightly higher than the left. How the skin around his eyes crinkled when he laughed.

"No kiss?" he asked.

She didn't want to kiss him. She ached to kiss him. How was that possible at the same time?

He took the decision from her as he leaned forward and softly touched her lips with his. Despite her best intentions to be unaffected, her whole body sort of melted against him, and when his arms went around her, she nearly wept. It was like coming home. But to a home made of nothing more than air.

His taste was familiar, and if she lived to be a hundred she'd never forget it. The way his back felt beneath her hands, the scent that was part soap, part male—all had become imprinted deep inside her. She never wanted to let him go. But she did. "I'd better go see about the twins." Before he had a chance to stop her, she was inside.

There were Jem and Scout, both of them still in pajamas, on the floor with cartoons blaring. The sight of them didn't help her situation. She'd dreamed of her unborn children. Her children with Gray.

Scout waved at her, and Shelby waved back. "You guys want scrambled eggs?"

"Okay," Scout said, turning to her show. Jem had no opinion. Scrambled eggs it was.

As she headed for the kitchen, she felt Gray behind her, and it was he who held open the swinging doors for her. She gave herself a strong, silent command to stop it. To enjoy the time she had left and quit wishing for things that could never be.

He headed for the coffeepot, and she took in a deep breath, then smiled. "You want to help?"

"Sure." He answered so fast she imagined he had been worried about her. Probably wondering what he'd done wrong.

"Okay. You take charge of the eggs. I've got other things to cook."

He sipped some coffee, gave her a heart-stopping grin and went to the cupboard. He brought out a Dutch oven instead of the frying pan, but he was so eager to help she didn't say a word.

"Six eggs," she said, "in a big bowl so you can whip them."

"Have they been bad?"

She laughed, and it was just what she needed. Laughter. She'd need her sense of humor if she was going to get through this. "Yes, they've been bad. So beat the hell out of them."

He got the correct bowl and the whisk, and neatly cracked all the eggs. In the meantime, she got out the dozen pears she was going to poach in red wine and Lattimer spices. When she turned to Gray again, he was indeed whipping the hell out of the eggs. "It's okay, cowboy," she said. "I think they've learned their lesson."

Jem walked in and climbed onto one of the dining room chairs. "Is breakfast ready?"

"No," Gray said. "So you have time to set the table."

"Me?"

"If I can make the eggs, you can set the table."

Jem's face scrunched in a look of utter trepidation. "*You're* making the eggs?"

"Yes, I am. And they're going to be the best eggs you've ever had."

Jem looked at Shelby and rolled his eyes. She

burst out laughing. What a hoot. Of course she didn't tell Gray what she was laughing about. Jem rewarded her with a dazzling smile.

From then on, breakfast went beautifully. The ache in her heart eased as she concentrated on the moment and not a second more. His laughter. The way he talked to Jem. The adorable way he asked her if the poached pears were part of breakfast.

"It's for dinner. Tonight."

"You don't have to do that."

"I know. But I want to."

He put his fork down. "Are you sure?"

"Tonight, we'll be Mr. and Mrs. Gray Jackson. We'll be charming, but people will notice a slight undercurrent between us. You'll get the job. I'll go home. You'll explain that it's better this way, then you'll go on to be the best marketing man in Texas. In time, you'll mention the divorce. Voilà."

He shook his head. "You've already done too much."

"It's okay. You don't have to worry. I'm an excellent actress. No one will suspect a thing."

"Can I go watch TV?" Scout asked.

Startled, Shelby nodded, and the twins took off. She hadn't meant to say so much in front of them. "I'm sorry."

"For what?"

"Talking about tonight while they were here. I wasn't thinking."

"I don't think they cared much."

"But you do."

He took her hand, doing that strange, wonderful thing to her insides.

"Shelby, I can't even believe I'm saying this, but what the hell. We've been honest all along. I'm not sure what this thing is between us. I mean, I don't know what's going to happen. What I can promise you."

"You don't have to promise me anything. I'm leaving tomorrow."

"I don't know how I feel about that."

She sighed as she squeezed his hand. "I don't, either."

"No?"

"You want honesty? Oh, God, I don't know if I'm brave enough."

"You are."

"All right. It's going to be very difficult to go. More than I ever could have imagined."

"You, too, huh?"

She swallowed, trying not to jump to conclusions. It didn't mean anything more than that they'd become friends. Friends who were great in bed together. "It's only been a few days, and yet I feel as if I've known you all my life. I'll miss you."

"It's not like you're going to the moon. I can be in Austin in a couple of hours," he told her.

"But with the new job—"

"If I get the new job."

"He can't do better. Lattimer's a smart man. He knows what he's found."

"I think he was more impressed with you than me."

"Nope. I may have fed him, but you showed him how he can make lots of money. Guess which one he thinks is more important?"

"I don't know. I hope so. I think on-line sales can

really make a difference. He's already in specialty catalogues, so he's got a built-in mailing list. And I was thinking… There's this Web site called Epicurious.com. I think we can cut a deal with them to feature his spices…."

She listened as he detailed more of his plan, but the words weren't nearly as important as the look in his eyes. His enthusiasm swept him up in a wave of innovation. There was no mistaking the way his posture changed, as if he was preparing for a long run. He needed to be here. He needed to succeed at this job. She was right to help out tonight. And she was right not to tell him she'd fallen completely in love with him.

CHAPTER SEVENTEEN

GRAY THREW the softball, an easy lob right into Jem's glove. Jem dropped it, but it wasn't the little guy's fault. The glove was too big, his body not quite mature enough to play catch with ease. "Good one, Jem. You had 'er."

Jem picked up the ball, which was bigger than his hand, and tossed it to Gray in a wildly uncoordinated overhand throw. Gray dashed right, but he wasn't fast enough. The ball landed with a thud on the green rye grass. He scooped it up in his brother's mitt. His was in a box in storage along with his other sports paraphernalia—skis, pool cue, basketball and a jersey once worn by Michael Jordan himself.

After he tossed another one to Jem, Gray looked at the house. At the porch. Shelby had gone inside. Probably just to get a drink or something. But then Scout came running out, a mitt on her hand, too. It was just as large as the one Jem used, and Gray decided that tomorrow, he'd go pick up a couple of junior mitts.

Scout nearly tripped in her effort to reach the fun. She had the mitt on backward, but that didn't stop her. "Throw it to me, Uncle Gray! Throw it!"

He glanced at the porch one more time before he attended to Scout. On his knees, he showed her how to put the mitt on. How to watch the ball all the time. He gave her a few other words of advice.

When he stood, he found himself searching for Shelby, wanting to hold up the game until he knew where she was. Half the pleasure of this outdoor playtime was seeing her face. Hearing her laugh. They were almost a family, the four of them. Borrowed, of course. But still, it felt real. He'd do this with his own kids one day. And Shelby? Well, Shelby would watch her husband and their kids.

"Uncle Gray!"

He spun to face Jem, who'd clearly grown impatient with his uncle's musings.

"Throw the ball!"

"Right. Sorry!" He walked a few feet from Scout. "You ready?"

She nodded, and he was close enough to her to see that she'd stuck out her tongue in her excitement. Man, it was great. He tossed the ball, and just as it approached Scout's mitt she turned her head away, squeezing her eyes shut. The ball landed a foot away. He thought she might be disappointed, but she wasn't. She just ran and got it, and threw it in that willy-nilly fashion of four-year-olds.

"That was excellent, Scout!"

Gray froze at the womanly voice from the porch. She was back, settling on the porch swing.

"I have hot cocoa and cookies when you're done."

He sighed, and his shoulders relaxed. She was here. "Why don't you come and play with us?"

She laughed and shook her mane of coppery hair. "Nope. I've got to watch the stove. I don't want anything to burn."

"The heck with the food. This is more important."

"You play," she said. "You do it so well."

He didn't try to force her. She might not be so great at it. A lot of girls weren't. She'd probably spent a lot more time in home ec than phys ed. He waved and got the ball. Jem started getting fancy with his throws, showing off for Scout. He went wild a couple of times and once nearly hit Gray in the eye. Shelby's laughter floated over the big back yard, and it made Gray want her. He wanted to make her laugh. He wanted to make her do all sorts of things.

After about half an hour, the kids got restless. Ellen had told him that at this age they had short attention spans, and she was right, but he wanted to keep playing. Not because he was so thrilled with catch. If he could wear them out, they'd take a nice, long nap, which would suit him just fine.

Another of Jem's throws went astray. Only it went the opposite direction this time, toward the porch. By the time Gray realized where the ball had gone, Shelby was already down the steps. She picked up the ball and tossed it gently in the air.

He stopped. Held his hand out. "Hey, lady, can we have our ball back?"

She turned to Scout. "What do you think?"

"No!"

"Yes!" Jem hollered at the same time.

"Hmm. Well, I guess I'll just go inside and bake this softball into a pie."

Scout found that hysterical, but Jem seemed a little worried.

"Hey, Jem," Gray called. "She's not going to bake it. She's going to throw it, right, Shelby?"

The woman in question gave an exaggerated sigh. "All right. But you have to go back."

"Back?"

"You want the ball?"

Gray took five steps backward.

"More."

"I'll be too far."

"More!"

He obeyed. The kids had both dropped their mitts, which Gray interpreted as the end of the game. But Shelby wasn't through yet.

"More."

"Jeez, Shelby, I'll be in Oklahoma."

"Just do it, baseball boy."

He grinned and gave her exactly what she wanted. He went *back*. If she'd been on the mound at Wrigley Field, he'd have been in center field. "Far enough?" he shouted.

She moved her right shoulder in a circle for a few rotations, then stretched her arm out and back. Finally, she nodded. Pulling back her arm, she hurled that baby straight to him. Straight to him! He even had to run back about a yard. The ball sailed into his glove with a satisfying smack.

He stared at the ball, then at Shelby. She was looking at a fingernail. "Hey!"

She looked up.

"Where'd you learn to do that?"

"Women's softball league. National championship, three years in a row."

"Holy sh—"

"Come on in, Scout. Jem," she said, saving their little ears from his epithet.

He shook his head as he walked toward the porch.

All that, and she could play baseball like Ken Griffey Jr. By the time he reached the porch, he'd fallen halfway in love.

SHE CLOSED the oven door and heard Gray walk into the kitchen. Before she could turn, he was behind her, close. Touching close. He put his hands on her waist and kind of shimmied. To say she understood his intentions immediately was something of an understatement. "Subtle, Jackson. Very subtle."

"But they're *asleep*."

"And?"

He spun her around. "Are you kidding? I've never slept with a woman who was better than me at baseball."

"It's very likely I'm better than you at a lot of things."

"Good. You can show me each and every one. Later. Now, I want to show you what I'm good at."

"Really. I'd never have guessed."

He kissed her, a playful smack on the lips, and then he grabbed her hand, pulling her away from the kitchen, away from the Asian lettuce pockets and the spiced Brie. Like a child pulling a red wagon behind him, he tugged and cajoled her all the way through the living room, down the hall and into his bedroom.

He smiled victoriously. "Gotcha."

That was the problem. He did have her. He had her and he didn't even know how much. She should have said no. In fact, she should have run the other way as fast as her legs would carry her. But she didn't. She just stood there, staring at him, her insides doing a tango.

His grin faltered as he took two more steps. His

finger went to her chin, and he tilted her head up a notch. Then he kissed her. And it was all over but the shouting.

HER HEAD rested on his shoulder and her hand was on his chest. The rapid beating of his heart echoed her own as they came down from the heady peak of the most intense lovemaking she'd ever dreamed of.

A quiver shook her body, and he must have felt it because he gave her arm a gentle squeeze. But they didn't speak. What would she have said? Not the truth. Not that her heart was breaking. That she'd been horribly wrong. If she'd known it would be this hard to say goodbye, she wouldn't have stayed.

It was the falling-in-love part that had ruined everything. If only she'd kept her heart to herself. She could have gone home a little more frustrated, but a lot happier.

She'd leave first thing tomorrow. And tonight, she'd sleep in the guest room. Not with Gray. She'd never sleep with Gray again. Even this time had been a mistake. The way they made love was too perfect. It made her future seem too empty.

"You okay?" he whispered.

"Sure."

"I'm not so hot."

She looked at him, but she couldn't see his face well. "Why not?"

He didn't answer her for a long time. Just as she was getting ready to prod him, he turned, moving her gently so they faced each other. His gorgeous gray eyes peered into hers, and she wasn't sure if the pain she saw was real or if it was a trick played by her desperate desire.

"This isn't turning out the way I planned," he said.

"What did you plan?"

"Not you. I could never have planned for you."

"Funny how that works, huh? I didn't plan on you, either."

"I keep reminding myself that Austin isn't that far away. Really, it's close. We'll see each other."

"Sure we will," she said, although she didn't believe it. He'd have his job, and that would take up so much of his time. There wasn't even a guarantee that he'd stay in Blue Point. Lattimer had said they were still looking for a new marketing headquarters. So if he moved to Los Angeles or New York, then what? She'd never see him again.

It was foolish to think this was any more than a dirt road off the main highway of her life. Everything she loved was in Austin. With the exception of the man rubbing her back.

"Thank you for tonight," he said.

"Tonight's not here yet."

"That's all right. I know you're going to be great. More than great. You're going to get me the job. I'm only afraid when they hear we're separating, Lattimer will think I'm such a dope he'll can me on the spot."

"You're sweet, but completely wrong."

"Gee, thanks."

"I mean that I'm not getting you anything. I'm quite certain you would have this job with or without me."

"No."

"In fact…"

His brows came down as if anticipating her decision.

"In fact, I think it's better that I don't go tonight."

"But—"

"Come on, Gray. We both know I don't need to be there. You can take the food with you."

"He thinks we're married."

"You can set him straight. It won't be a big deal unless you make it one."

"I don't want you to leave."

She nodded, but then she had to turn away. She didn't want him to see her cry. "I'd better call the baby-sitter," she said as she tossed the covers aside.

His hand gripped her arm. "Don't go."

"I have to."

She waited for him to convince her. To give her a reason to stay. He didn't.

She got out of bed and hurried to the bathroom, locking the door behind her. The hot water in the shower mingled with her tears. The worst part of it was what an idiot she'd been. How she could have let herself fall so utterly in love with a man she knew she couldn't have. But now it was too late. She couldn't turn off her feelings any more than she could go back in time. She'd have to live with this mistake forever, one long day after the next. Always wishing it could have turned out differently.

She took her time with her makeup, careful to disguise her red-rimmed eyes. When she found herself redoing her hair for the third time, she realized she was stalling. She wanted to throw a tantrum and make things work out her own way, but at the same time she was very aware of the childishness of her reaction. He'd touched that part of her, the child, as well as the woman. That wasn't something she'd expected. No one among her friends had told her he would reawaken the kid inside her. That he'd engage her on so many levels. Why couldn't it have been just sex? Was that so much to ask?

She left the bathroom. Gray wasn't there. She took the opportunity to get the phone book and call the woman from the baby shop. The arrangements were made in a few minutes, and then there were no more excuses left.

CHAPTER EIGHTEEN

GRAY CHECKED on the kids. They were still sleeping, but he knew that wouldn't last. They never slept more than an hour in the afternoon, and even though he'd worn them out, they weren't going to break the pattern today.

He softly closed the door then went to the guest bathroom and gathered his toiletries. He'd showered there, not wanting to disturb Shelby. Actually, he had wanted to disturb her. He'd almost joined her in the bathroom. Twice, he'd put his hand on the door-knob. But in the end, he realized he needed to let her be. She was leaving. That was all there was to it. So what if he didn't want her to go? It was just another example of his selfishness. Never mind what was right for Shelby. She should leave her home, her business, her life and come with him because he wanted her to. Jeez. He really was a selfish bastard.

A sound from downstairs told him Shelby was in the kitchen. He hurried down the stairs, made a quick detour to his room to drop off his things, then headed straight for her. Maybe she'd changed her mind. Maybe—

Her bag was by the front door.

His pace slowed until he'd stopped completely. His only consolation was that he'd be so busy with the new job he wouldn't have time to think about her. If he got the job. If he didn't, that meant he had to keep looking. Maybe he could find something in Austin.

Why hadn't he thought of that before? Of course! He didn't *have* to take this job. It wasn't as if he was going to get to live near his family even if he got the job. The new marketing office was going to be in Dallas or Houston. Lattimer Spices was just another company. He hadn't even looked in Austin.

He pushed through the swinging doors and found Shelby putting one of her concoctions into a plastic container. She jumped when she heard him, staring at him with big, wounded eyes. The smile that came a few seconds later was as fake as a three-dollar bill. She'd smile for real when he told her his plan.

"I'm almost done with these," she said. "I found a box in the utility room, so the food won't get all over your car."

"That's great," he said. "But here's what I was thinking."

She stopped, her hand in midair. "What?"

"I'm not going to take the job."

"Pardon me?"

"I said I'm not going to take it. I'm going to look for a job in Austin."

She didn't move for a long second, then she closed her eyes. A few seconds after that she opened them again. "Thank you," she whispered. "But no."

"No?"

She put the food down and walked over to him. She stood just out of his reach. "You need to take the job, Gray."

"Why? There are others. There must be a company in Austin that needs a man like me."

"I'm sure there are several. That doesn't mean you should go."

"Why not? Shelby, I don't want to lose you."

"I know. I don't want to lose you, either, but you have something important to do here. I don't want you losing sight of that."

"I'm not."

"No? What was it you said you were afraid of? That I'd distract you. I'd say not taking the job and looking for something in Austin is pretty strong evidence of distraction, wouldn't you?"

"No," he said, but the moment he said it, doubt hit him hard. What if she was right? What if—

"I've called the sitter. She's coming at six. She'll give the kids dinner. I've left you the directions to Lattimer's house." She pointed to the counter. "By the phone."

He walked toward her. "Isn't there anything I can say?"

"Yes. You can tell me it's been wonderful. You can tell me we'll always be friends."

"You know that's true."

She smiled, and this time there was honest pleasure mixed with sadness. He understood completely. "You're going to be great," she said, her voice catching slightly. "You're going to put Lattimer Spices on the map."

"I hope so."

She touched his cheek with her fingers, then her palm. He closed his eyes, soaking up her warmth. There had to be a way.

"There's something else I want to tell you."

He opened his eyes to find her gaze on him. "What?"

"Your mother is proud of you. Right now. You don't have to do anything more. I never knew her, but I can promise you this. She loved you for exactly who you are. All she wanted, all she still wants, is for you to find happiness and peace within yourself. I think she would be happy about the job, but probably not for the reasons you think. I think she sees what I see. A man with unlimited potential. A man with a generous heart and a loving spirit. A man she'd be proud to love."

His throat constricted, and he had to clear it to talk. "Shelby—"

"I know."

"No, you don't."

She leaned over and kissed him gently on the mouth. "I do." After she stepped away, he could see unshed tears glisten in her beautiful eyes. "I've left my Austin number by the phone. Call me sometime."

"Aren't you going to say goodbye to the twins?"

She shook her head. "Give them my love, would you? Tell them how much I've enjoyed getting to know them."

"They'll miss you."

"I—" She turned abruptly and walked through the swinging doors of the kitchen.

Gray stood alone, knowing he shouldn't let her go. What they had was something special. Something he might never find again. Only one thing stopped him. He wasn't sure. Not absolutely. Not one hundred percent. There was no doubt that he cared for Shelby more than any woman he'd ever known. But was it love? Was he subconsciously using his feelings for Shelby to run away?

He had to find out for sure. He had to stay, get the job, chart his course. Then he could go after her. It would be difficult, but he couldn't risk something this important.

The sound of the front door closing was like a physical blow. He shot out of the kitchen and ran to the front door, yanking it open so hard the entry shuddered. He ran toward her car, desperate to stop her. But she must not have seen him waving as her car sped down the drive. He didn't stop, though. He kept on waving until her car had disappeared from sight.

The overwhelming feeling that he'd just made the biggest mistake of his life kept him outside for who knew how long. It was only when Jem came out to see what was wrong that Gray realized what he'd been doing.

"Shelby had to go home," he told the boy as they walked into the house together.

"She didn't say goodbye."

"She wanted to. She was really upset that you guys weren't awake. But she asked me to tell you that she liked you both a lot. That she'd think about you all the time."

Jem climbed onto the couch, his eyelids still heavy from his nap. "She was nice."

"Yeah, she was."

He frowned the way kids do, with all his feelings right there on his face. "Did she cook dinner?"

Gray burst out laughing, but quickly stifled it as he saw the confusion on Jem's face. "No, she didn't. But someone just as nice is going to come to stay with you tonight. Her name is Sarah DeWitt, and she's been with you guys before."

"Is she the old lady?"

"I'm not sure. We'll see when she gets here."

"Okay."

"Where's Scout?"

Jem shrugged, then picked up the television remote. As he searched for cartoons, the phone rang, and Gray headed for the kitchen, hoping it was Shelby. Hoping she'd tell him she made a mistake. "Hello?"

"Gray."

"Hey, Ben," he said, forcing himself to forget about Shelby, at least for now. "How's Ellen?"

"Good news, Gray. Maybe the best news ever. She's fine. She's wonderful."

He could hear the relief in his brother's voice, and for the first time in his life he completely understood. He'd been jealous of Ellen for a long time, even though he liked her. It was just that Ben changed so much after they met. His brother had been totally into sports—a weekend warrior, playing on local softball and basketball teams. They'd done a lot of that together, and then Ellen had come along and that was the end of it.

Now Gray got it. Better late than never. "I'm really glad for you, Ben. I mean it. It's terrific."

"I know. I don't mind confessing that I was scared. Really scared. I don't know what I'd do without her."

"I know," Gray said.

"Are you all right?"

"Yeah. Yeah, sure. It's just—"

"What? Are the kids okay?"

"Oh, man, yes. I didn't mean to scare you. They're fine."

"Then what is it?"

"The woman who was here helping out for the last few days—she just left."

"And?"

"And I really didn't want her to go."

Ben didn't say anything for a moment. "Uh, isn't she pregnant?"

"No. Not her. She had her baby a couple of days ago. I mean Shelby. You don't know her. She's from Austin. She showed up looking for her mother. Then she...stayed."

"Ellen tells me I'm the least intuitive person on planet Earth, but are you telling me you went into heat with the baby-sitter?"

"It wasn't like that."

"What was it like?"

"I don't know. I mean, it can't happen this fast, can it? In a few days?"

Another long pause. Gray thought about telling his brother it was all a joke, but just as he opened his mouth, Ben said, "It happened to me, little brother."

"What?"

"I fell for Ellen in two seconds flat. Oh, I fought it for a while, but what was it the woman said in that movie? She had me at hello."

"I'm not in love with Shelby."

"Are you sure?"

"No."

"I figured it would happen one day. That you'd get tired of all those starving girls in their convertibles. I just didn't think it would happen this soon."

"I'm not saying it has."

"Tell me one thing. Are you still interviewing for that job?"

"Yeah. I'm going to Lattimer's house tonight for dinner."

"Then I'd say you don't have anything to worry about."

"What does that mean?"

"If you'd told me you were going to pass on the job and follow this gal to wherever she's from, I'd say it wasn't about her at all, but about you."

Gray coughed, hardly believing he was so transparent. Had everyone in his family been able to see through him?

"Gray?"

"Yeah."

"Don't do anything stupid, okay? We're coming home tomorrow. We'll talk. We'll figure the whole damn thing out, and then some."

"Right."

"And, Gray?"

"What?"

"You're gonna do great."

Gray shook his head. "Thanks for the encouragement, but I'm fine. Stop worrying. Just go take care of that wife of yours, would you? I'll see you tomorrow."

"Don't tell the kids, okay? We want to surprise them."

"You got it. Oh, and, Ben?"

"Yeah."

"Little brother, my ass."

Ben laughed as Gray hung up the phone. He stood there staring at nothing, thinking about what his brother had said. Could it be possible? Did he love Shelby Lord?

He'd never felt this way before, that was for sure.

But love? Did love hurt like this? Did it make a person crazy, not knowing what in hell to do?

He shouldn't have let her go. At least not until he figured this thing out. Maybe it wasn't love, but it could become love. Maybe all he had to do was get the job and things would fall into place.

Damn it. Why did everything have to be all or nothing with him? He thought about what Shelby had said about his mother being happy with him, and his own belief that he'd been a selfish ass forever.

Had he really been that? Or had he just known he wasn't ready for a commitment? For children. He'd have been irresponsible to pretend he was. Of course, he could have handled himself better, that was a given, but hey, didn't he get points for seeing that? For knowing his limitations?

He knew something else now. That he wasn't a kid anymore. He was ready to move on with his life. To find happiness in a home, in a family. In a wife.

He pulled out his wallet and dug for Shelby's cell phone number. He was so anxious, it took two tries to punch it in. After four rings he was about to give up, but then her voice mail came on. He hesitated, not really wanting to leave a message. "Ah, hell. Shelby? Where are you?" He sighed. "I know where you should be. Here. Getting ready for Lattimer's party. I thought a lot about what you said.... We can make it, Shelby. We can have it all. I know we— Damn it, this isn't the way I wanted to say this. I hate this machine. Call me when you get to Austin and—"

The machine cut him off.

It was definitely time for a beer. He pulled one out of the fridge and unscrewed the top, then headed to the living room. Scout was on the couch with Jem, both of them staring silently as a cartoon ghost turned a cat into a cow.

He sat down right between them. The cow had turned back into a cat, although Gray wasn't sure why. He sipped his beer. Stared at the set. But mostly, he missed Shelby.

The ghost had started to pick on a pony when Scout scooted over and leaned against him. He put his arm around her, and she snuggled close, pulling her little legs up on the couch. A moment later, and Jem had moved to his other side.

He couldn't drink his beer like this. Not with the kids so close. Not with his arms holding them. But it didn't matter. He just settled back and watched that crazy ghost get in all sorts of mischief.

The only thing missing was Shelby.

CHAPTER NINETEEN

GRAY PARKED his Z-3 in front of Lattimer's house, but he didn't get out. The place was huge, a mansion more than a home. A large expanse of perfectly manicured lawn dotted with stately trees led up to an antebellum porch, complete with colonnades. Silhouettes at the windows showed him a much larger crowd than he'd anticipated. Shelby had been right to make so many hors d'oeuvres.

He wished she was here. It would have made everything easier. Not that he didn't think he could do a good job with Lattimer, but being with Shelby automatically gave him points. Her restaurant must have lots of regulars. He'd like to see her there, floating from table to table, making her patrons feel at ease and welcome.

It was time. He climbed out of the car and got the big box of food from the back. It was a short walk from the gravel parking area to the front door. Just as he balanced the box on his knee to ring the bell, the door swung open. A young woman smiled at him. "You must be Gray Jackson."

He nodded. "Guilty."

"I'm Jessica Lattimer. Please come in. Daddy's been expecting you."

He followed the attractive young woman into the bright lights of the foyer. The house was more beautiful inside than even he would have guessed. Italian marble on the floor, a staircase worthy of Tara, and art that would have made the most savvy collector drool.

Jessica, who looked to be in her late teens, led him past the staircase, through the empty dining room and into a kitchen that was as big as his last apartment. The Lattimers must throw some wild dinner parties.

A whole gaggle of catering folk were knee deep in food preparation. He wondered how they were going to take to him bringing his own, as it were.

"You can put that here," Jessica said, nodding toward a large butcher block table. "We're all looking forward to seeing what you've brought."

He set down the box, and just as he was about to start unloading it, a white-coated chef stepped in and took over. Jessica smiled, showing even white teeth. Her blond hair shimmered in the overhead light. Her diamond earrings did, too. He'd bet the farm they were real.

"I imagine you can use a drink," she said. "Why don't we go out and find Daddy, and I'll make sure you have a cocktail in a heartbeat."

"Thank you," he said, liking her southern accent and her southern charm. She was going to break some hearts. She probably already had.

Again, he followed her, this time into the midst of the party. Waiters carried trays expertly through the considerable crowd. Gray figured there must be at least sixty people milling about. He didn't recognize anyone, which was to be expected. He heard Lattimer's booming laugh, but he didn't spot him right away. Jessica smiled charmingly at the guests as they followed the sound. Finally, he could see Lattimer towering over the group he held in thrall.

"What can I bring you?" Jessica asked. "The martinis are particularly good, I understand."

"Great," he said. "Thank you."

"My pleasure."

He watched her walk away, then turned his attention to Lattimer. The big man was laughing again, and the nearer Gray got, the more raucous the laughter became. Only he didn't think it was Lattimer who was holding court. Not from his reaction. Someone else held the floor. Perhaps Lattimer's wife?

Lattimer saw him before he reached the small crowd. "Gray Jackson. I was wondering what time you were going to get here."

"I had to make a delivery first. A whole box full."

"Excellent! I, for one, am going to excuse myself and investigate. And if you folks are wise, you'll follow me, because these treats won't last."

He headed toward the kitchen, and one by one the guests followed him. Mostly, they were Lattimer's age. Well coifed, exuberantly jeweled. It was a tony crowd, and he'd guess that most of them had homes like this, had lives like this, had roots like Lattimer's. It was a lifestyle he didn't know well, but it appealed to him. Not so much the money, although that was great, but the sense of belonging. Of knowing where you'd been and where you were going.

He thought about following Lattimer, but Jessica was coming with his drink. He'd wait, then go see their reaction to Shelby's food. He'd call her tomorrow, or maybe the next day, and give her a full report. It was a shame she couldn't be here to see it herself.

As he was turning to find Jessica, a man approached him as if he were an old friend. "Gray Jackson, I assume?"

"Yes, sir."

He held out his hand. "Carl Beckwith."

Gray shook his hand, liking the man right away for his easy smile and relaxed air. He was the vice-president and CFO of Lattimer Spices, one of the men who would have to approve Gray's getting the job.

"It's good to meet you. Jim speaks highly of you."

"That's nice to hear. I'd like to work with him."

Carl nodded as if it was a done deal. But Gray wasn't so sure. He wasn't counting on a thing until he'd signed on the dotted line.

"I was just talking to your lovely wife. She's a charming woman, and I dare say she'll be an asset to the Lattimer Spices family."

"My wife?"

Beckwith looked at him strangely, then turned his gaze toward the side of the room where Lattimer had been moments before. The crowd had gone, all except one.

She wore a black dress that showed her curves, high heels that showed her gorgeous legs. Her red hair swung loose around her shoulders. Her smile lit him up like a Christmas tree.

He remembered to excuse himself from Beckwith, which was something of a miracle, because the whole rest of the world disappeared from his gaze. All he could see was Shelby.

"Hi," she said.

"Hi."

"I decided to come to the party."

"So I see." He didn't touch her. Not because he didn't want to, but because he wasn't sure she wouldn't vanish in a cloud of smoke.

"I hope you don't mind."

"No. I don't mind."

"Thank goodness."

He drank in the sight of her. The scent of her sweet perfume. The way her eyes danced with humor and grace. All he wanted was to take her in his arms. But if he did, he'd never let go. "What made you change your mind?"

"I'm not sure, really. The car just sort of turned around. And then I was at the mall, and there was this dress. I couldn't resist, and then it occurred to me that I had the perfect place to wear the dress."

"It's beautiful."

"Thank you. It was on sale."

"You're beautiful."

"I missed you."

He grinned, teasing. "Not me. I haven't thought of you at all."

She stepped closer to him. Close enough to make his whole body hum with desire. "I don't believe you."

"Smart woman." He leaned ever so slightly, his mouth close to her ear. "Come with me."

She closed her eyes for a few seconds, which he took as a yes. He started walking toward the staircase, toward a bathroom he'd seen briefly on his way in. Out of the corner of his eye he spotted Jessica with his martini. He walked faster, quickly guiding Shelby around the corner to the foyer. Her high heels clicked on the marble, making him picture her slim ankles, her long legs.

The bathroom was vacant. He took a quick glance to make sure no one was watching. A waiter popped out of the dining room just as Gray took her hand and pulled her inside.

The second the door was closed, he pushed her against it, pressed his hands to the door on either side of her head and kissed her. Kissed her well and proper. After, he looked deeply into her eyes. "I thought I'd lost you."

"I know."

"I'm not sure—"

"I know," she said again. Then she smiled. "Maybe we're not supposed to be sure."

"I don't ever want to hurt you. Not for anything."

She touched his face with her fingers, and he closed his eyes, savoring the feeling. "I know that, too."

"So what are we going to do?"

"I don't know about later." She leaned forward and teased his lips with her teeth. "But I can think of something really interesting for right now."

He didn't need any more prodding. She moaned as he thrust his tongue inside her warmth. She tasted so damn good. So hot. He rubbed against her, showing her how much he'd missed her. How much he wanted her.

Her hands went to his chest, lingered there for a moment, then moved slowly down as his kisses grew more urgent. When she touched his belt, he pulled his head back, grimacing with the effort to slow down, to stop the imminent explosion. Of course, it got worse as her hand moved down, as she rubbed his hard length.

"I can't stand it," he said, his voice a low growl.

"What?" she asked. Then she squeezed him with just enough pressure to drive him insane. "This?"

"Stop."

"Stop? You mean you don't like it when I do this?"

He growled again and ran his hands down her back to just below her behind. In one quick move he lifted her, forcing a small yelp from her lips as she grasped his shoulders for balance. He put her on the long bathroom counter. His hands went to her knees, and as he spread her legs, her dress inched up her thighs until he could see the tops of her stockings.

Fascinated, he pushed the dress up a little more. She wasn't wearing panty hose. Instead, she had on silk stockings held up by a black lace garter belt. He moaned as the image became branded in his brain. His fingers went to the tops of her thighs, and he ran his thumbs over the edge of the material. She arched her back as his hands crept higher, lifting her dress, revealing the soft, pale flesh just above the stockings.

He touched silk. The leg bands of her panties. He took her mouth once more as he slipped his thumbs underneath the material. As she teased him with her tongue, he returned the favor, but in a far more sensitive spot. She moaned again, and he felt her readiness.

It was no good. He couldn't stand it another second. He unzipped his pants, freed his aching erection, and in one long stroke he was all the way inside her.

Her fingers gripped his shoulders so hard he could feel her nails through his jacket. He held her hips and pulled her forward until she was at the very edge of the counter.

He locked onto her gaze as he thrust in and out, slowly at first, then faster and faster. She breathed heavily, but she never shut her eyes, and neither did he. They were connected, and not just at their sex. He was in her, and with her, and she was in him. Nothing in his life had prepared him for this. Nothing.

She squeezed him, thrust her pelvis forward, and that was it. He couldn't stand it another second. He wanted to cry out, to roar with his release. Instead, he kissed her once more, and when he came, he felt her tremble with her own climax.

It felt like he was suspended in time, at this perfect moment. This was where he belonged. Inside her.

Finally, time began again, and she slumped forward, laying her head on his shoulder. "Oh, my."

"I'll say."

"I sure hope no one had to use the bathroom."

"I'm sure there's more than one."

"Right."

He struggled to slow his breathing, and although he didn't want to, he had to move. "Stay still," he whispered after he kissed her lips. He turned on the water, got it nice and warm. The next few minutes were intimate and shocking as they realized what they'd done.

She straightened her dress, then ran a hand through her hair. "All I need is lipstick," she said, "and no one will be the wiser."

He took her in his arms one last time. "All I need is you."

"Nothing's changed."

"That's where you're wrong." He kissed her hard, then led her out of the bathroom. They got to the living room just in time to hear Lattimer announce dinner.

Gray held her hand as they walked into the elaborately decorated dining room. Whoever had arranged the seating chart was officially going into his will as he found his name next to Shelby's. Shelby Jackson. Everyone was still under the impression they were married.

He pulled out the seat for her, then as he scooted the chair in, he leaned close to her ear. "Do you trust me?"

She nodded without hesitation.

He sat next to her. On his other side was an elderly woman who turned out to be Lattimer's mother. She was nice enough, but almost deaf, so Gray had to speak much more loudly than he'd have liked.

He checked with Shelby often, but she was busy in conversation with the man on her left, Carl Beckwith. The dinner began with Shelby's Asian lettuce wraps, which everyone approved of. In fact, they were gone in a flash. Wine was poured, then a salad of spring greens, sun-dried tomatoes and goat cheese was served with a balsamic vinaigrette. Their secret simmered between them, and it amazed him that the dinner went on in its usual manner. Polite chitchat, a laugh here and there. Couldn't they see? Wasn't it obvious by the brightness of her eyes, the way she smiled?

He touched her thigh, and she blushed. But a few

moments later, her fingers were on his thigh. The mischief in her gaze warned him to expect the worst, and sure enough, her hand went where it shouldn't have. At least not then.

She laughed, but it wasn't at him. Beckwith had said something amusing. So amusing, her hand disappeared, leaving him in a highly agitated state.

He sipped some wine while he thought about baseball scores, but that only lasted for a few moments. Then he thought about what it would be like tomorrow. And the day after that. All the days ahead of him without Shelby. The picture was dull, black and white, lonely. If he'd never met her, that would be one thing, but he had, and he couldn't go back. She'd changed everything.

He looked at Lattimer, who happened to be watching him. The man who would be his boss smiled, lifted his brow and nodded at Shelby. Gray smiled back, understanding exactly what the older man was getting at. She wasn't your ordinary, run-of-the-mill woman. Not by a long shot. She was bright, funny, talented, perceptive. What kind of a fool would let a woman like her get away?

They'd only known each other five days. Five days! It seemed impossible that he could love her. But if love meant that he wanted to spend the rest of his life getting to know everything about her, he had fallen. Fallen hard. To wake up to her smile. To watch her grow with their children. To be there for her to lean on. Nothing could be more important than that. Not this job. Not any job.

The waiter came with the next course, filet mignon with wild mushrooms and saffron rice. Mrs. Lattimer spoke to him as he ate, hardly tasting a thing. And yet he managed to carry on the conversation. How, he didn't know. His head was fairly bursting with his revelation, and the need to tell Shelby.

She listened to Carl as he went on about his daughter, Paula. Seems Paula was a chef, just graduated from the Culinary Institute of America. Carl asked Shelby's advice about finding a job, and she told him what she could.

"Where did you go to school?"

"I've taken some classes in Austin, at a private school there."

"You're all Jim's talked about for days. You and that young husband of yours."

She stole a glance at Gray. He'd heard. So had most of the people at the table. His gaze caught hers, and with one look her heart started beating so hard she thought it might burst. He was up to something, and she prayed she'd guessed what.

She still could hardly believe what they'd done in the bathroom, or that she'd come here. But the farther she had driven from Blue Point, the more depressed she'd been. Almost without her permission, the car had turned back. She'd found herself in this dress, knowing she was about to do one of two things—make the biggest, most humiliating mistake a woman could make or find herself in the arms of the man she loved.

All her adult life, she'd wanted one thing more than any other. To love a man unconditionally, and to be loved in return. It was the only thing that made sense to her, the only reason to be here, on this journey called life. To find her other half. To have children together. To be companions, friends, lovers.

If only this dinner was over! She would tell him.

Tell him everything. How much she loved him, how she'd give up her life in Austin for him, because without him there was no life for her. Now she wondered if she could wait till after dinner. She might have to steal him away, company or no company.

She took a bite of food, mostly to be polite. She wasn't hungry. Her stomach was filled with butterflies. She smiled at Carl, then heard the distinctive sound of silver on crystal, a clear high tone ringing across the table. She turned to Lattimer, who held a fork next to his wineglass. The guests quieted, and the big man stood.

"Thank you all for being here tonight. Nothing's more important in this world than family and friends. I consider each one of you one or the other, and some of you both. Tonight we have two special guests. Gray Jackson, born and raised in Blue Point, and his wife, Shelby, the magnificent cook who graced us with the best of the hors d'oeuvres. Thank you, Shelby."

She smiled, nodded, feeling her cheeks heat as he spoke of her as Gray's wife. She didn't want to play this game anymore.

"I want to welcome Gray not only to our circle of friends and family, but to our company. If he accepts the position, he'll be our new vice-president in charge of worldwide marketing."

Everyone clapped at the announcement. Everyone but Shelby. She turned to Gray, thrilled for him, but scared, so scared.

Gray smiled at her. Then he stood up. "Thank you, Jim. Thank you all. I'm honored, not only to be here, but to have such a wonderful offer. I'd love to accept you right here and now, only..." He looked at Shelby again. "Only there's been a mis-understanding. My fault. I should have corrected this several days ago. The beautiful woman on my left isn't my wife. In fact, we only met five days ago. She came to my brother's house searching for her past. I shamelessly cajoled her into staying and help-ing me with my niece and nephew."

Shelby couldn't breathe. The rest of the room got hazy, and the only thing clear and vibrant was Gray.

"It was the single smartest thing I've ever done. She's not my wife. At least, not yet."

Shelby grew dizzy as Gray stepped away from his chair to stand behind her. He shifted her chair so they were facing each other, then he lowered himself to one knee. He took her right hand in his, kissed her palm, then looked into her eyes. "Shelby Lord, I've fallen madly in love with you. I didn't mean for it to happen, but it did. And now I can't conceive of going through another day without you by my side. Would you do me the honor of becoming my wife?"

Shelby's hand shook so hard she almost knocked him in the teeth. She didn't trust her voice at all. "Yes," she whispered. "Yes, and yes, and yes."

He bowed his head for a long moment. And when he looked up again, looked into her eyes, she couldn't stop the tears from welling in them.

"I think this calls for a toast," Jim Lattimer said.

Gray stood up and pulled her into his arms. He kissed her softly, reverently. "Thank you," he said for her ears only.

Lattimer lifted his wineglass. "To the happy cou-ple."

"To the happy couple!"

Glasses clinked, wine was drunk, and Shelby

touched his face with her hand. "Just checking," she said.

"Checking?"

She nodded. "To make sure you're real. That this isn't a dream."

"You're my dream," he said, then he kissed her again.

A masculine cough parted them. With Gray's arm around her waist, she turned to Jim Lattimer once more.

"The job offer still stands, Gray."

"I have to discuss it with my fiancée."

"Well, discuss this. What say we talk about moving the marketing headquarters to, say, Austin?"

Gray's mouth opened, and Shelby laughed out loud.

"And if you play your cards right," the big man said, "maybe you can convince that fiancée of yours to be a consultant to the test kitchen."

"I'll do my best, sir."

"That's all a man can hope for."

"I respectfully disagree." Gray kissed her once more. "*She's* all a man can hope for."

"Hear, hear," someone said. But Shelby wasn't listening. The only person who existed was Gray. The man she loved, and who loved her in return. The man she would grow old with. Her companion, her friend, her lover.

EPILOGUE

One year later

SHELBY HAD TO sit down. She didn't want to. The party was just getting into full swing. But she wasn't the only one making the decisions these days. Three little ones, eight and a half months old and still inside her, had the biggest vote. And they wanted her to sit.

She put her hand on her belly, so big it seemed impossible. She felt them move, but that wasn't new. At least one of them was going to be a flamenco dancer. She just wished he would stop using her bladder as his practice floor.

Maybe it wasn't a he. Maybe the dancer was their little girl. It didn't matter. They were all three healthy, and in a very short time they would be in her arms.

She felt a cool hand on her shoulder. "Are you all right?"

She looked up to see Gray, concern forcing his brows down. "Yes. I'm fine. Go on. I'll be up and about soon."

"I'd rather stay here with you."

"It's your party."

He sighed, then pulled a chair close to her. His gaze traveled the hotel banquet room, decorated to the nines in celebration of Lattimer Spices' record third quarter. To say Gray's marketing plans had been a success was an understatement. They'd become the most purchased condiments on the Internet, with worldwide sales in the millions.

He turned to her. "Wow, huh?"

She nodded. "I'll say. Oh, Ben and Ellen here yet?"

He shook his head. "I'm expecting them any minute. Kate, too."

"I bet the twins have sprouted again."

"I wouldn't be surprised."

"Oh, my. That was a hard kick."

"Can I get you anything?"

"No. Just tell me how much you love me."

He grinned. "I told you that an hour ago."

"So, what have you done for me lately?"

He laughed as Jim Lattimer joined them. "How are you and the triplets, Shelby?"

"We're all hanging in here."

"This is a hell of a shindig. You sure know how to throw a party, missy."

"I didn't do it. Mary Jane and Lacy did most of the work. I just nodded a few times."

"You can't fool me. This has your fingerprints all over it."

She smiled. "Thanks, Jim. For everything."

"Don't thank me. All I've done is sit back and make money."

"Have you met Megan Maitland yet? And my brothers and sister?"

"I've met Garrett. Good man. I liked him right off."

"He's a sweetie. Too worried about me, but then, I guess that's what brothers are for."

"Seems to me you're surrounded by folks worried about you."

She shifted on her chair, trying to get comfortable. Of course, that was hopeless, so she got busy looking at the guests. A lot of them were business associates, of course, but there were many of her friends here. Abby and Kyle. Darcy and Mitch. Connor and Lacy. Mary Jane and Morgan. Ford and Katie Carrington. Drake Logan and Hope. Anna and Jake and Beth and Ellie and their mates... Everyone she loved. Just then her brother Michael walked in, Jenny on his arm. Lana followed him with Dylan.

"I—" She stopped as a cramp hit her hard.

"Shelby?" Gray was on his feet. "What is it?"

"I—" Another one. Bigger this time. "I think we're going to have to leave the party, sweetie."

"What?"

"I'm not positive, but I think I'm in labor."

Gray's face paled, and he swayed a bit. Lattimer put a beefy hand on his shoulder. "Get a grip, man. Then get the car."

"Right. Grip. Car."

"Gray, honey?"

"Yes?"

"It's not enough to say it. You actually have to get the car."

"Right." He leaned over, kissed her, stood straight, shook Lattimer's hand, then promptly walked into a waiter carrying a whole tray of drinks. The commotion seemed to help motivate him, and he ran out of the room.

Everyone was staring at her. Murmuring. Moving

in for a better look. Guess this wasn't the kind of thing she could keep a secret. "Surprise," she said, and then she had no more interest in the guests at all. She gripped her stomach as the contraction hit.

When she looked up, Mitchell, Abby, Ford and Megan—the top staff at Maitland maternity—surrounded her. "Boy, if there was ever a place to go into labor, this is it."

Mitchell took one hand, Ford the other, and they helped raise her to her feet. She felt very much like a beached whale, but this probably wasn't the time to be concerned about that. The guests cleared a path for her, and she smiled as brightly as she could, given the circumstances.

Gray met them at the door. His eyes were as wide as saucers, his cheeks flushed. It was a good thing they were only two blocks from the hospital. Even he could manage to get her there safely.

"I'll take it from here," he said. Then he put his arm around what was left of her waist and grabbed her hand. He looked behind him. "Abby?"

"What, Gray?"

"Why are you still here?"

"Sorry. I'll see you at the clinic."

"Thank you."

Shelby chuckled as Abby dashed in front of them. Gray held her firmly, comforting her with the strength of his loving arms. This was it. They were actually going to be parents tonight. Two little boys, one little girl. Cody, Luke and Nora Jackson.

They reached the car, and Gray helped her in. Another contraction hit as Gray got into the car. They were coming awfully fast.

She wasn't sure how, and she had a feeling it was

better that she didn't know, but they reached Maitland Maternity in about a minute and a half. Abby was there with a wheelchair. Gray helped her out of the car and got her seated. He kissed her, and she grabbed his hand, holding him still.

"What's wrong?"

"Nothing."

"But—"

His impatience nearly made her skip it. But no. She wouldn't. It was too important. "I just want to tell you something."

"What?" he asked.

"You're the best thing that's ever happened to me. I love you with all my heart."

"Yeah, me, too. Now go on. Get inside. I don't want you having the babies here in the ambulance bay."

She smiled, even through the next contraction. Gray's cavalier response didn't faze her in the least. He showed her his love every single day. He'd blossomed with the job, with the marriage. Together, they were happier than either one of them had been alone. Happier than any two people had a right to be. And now this.

He walked by her side into the clinic and up to her room. And he stayed with her all during the long, difficult afternoon and night.

And he was there with her when each one of their precious children was born. Weeping with joy, he carried Nora and put her on Shelby's chest. Then he came back with the boys.

It was the most perfect moment of her life. Gray kissed her, and their tears mingled on her cheek.

"I love you." His voice cracked with emotion, but

he cleared his throat and went on. "What you said to me before? It's more than true for me. You're my reason to live. You're everything. You, and now them."

"It must be..." she said.

"What?"

"Fate."

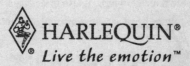
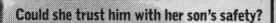

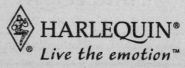

Forrester Square

LEGACIES . LIES . LOVE .

Coming in April 2004...
a brand-new Forrester Square tale!

ILLEGALLY YOURS

by favorite
Harlequin American Romance® author

JACQUELINE DIAMOND

Determined to stay in America despite an
expired visa, pregnant Kara Tamaki turned to
attorney Daniel Adler for help. Daniel wasn't an
immigration lawyer, but he knew how to help
Kara stay in America—marry her!

Forrester Square...Legacies. Lies. Love.

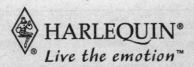

HARLEQUIN®
Live the emotion™